GABE

FEDERAL PROTECTION AGENCY

BOOK EIGHT

BY EVIE RILEY

GABE

An investigation goes awry.
Their world gets turned upside down.
Embers ignite in close proximity.

FBI Agent Gabe Long finds himself reluctantly assigned to keep an eye on Sebastian Roth after the detective meets with a couple of too-related-to-be-coincidental "accidents." He isn't too happy about having to play babysitter to a stubborn, impulsive, and relentless investigator who won't let go of a dangerous pedophile ring case, but the man has clearly gotten himself into some hot water.

Frankie Zolnai is a skilled physical therapist known for his compassion and commitment to his patients. His warm smile and gentle demeanor create a safe space for those in need of healing. At the request of his best friend, Newt, Frankie agrees to provide PT to Sebastian after an accident leaves Sebastian injured.

Gabe and Frankie's paths cross and as the two connect over their shared medical knowledge, sparks fly. As the two men get to know each other, Gabe reveals things about his past very few people know. Frankie quickly becomes a person Gabe can count on to be there—a rare thing for Gabe.

Gabe wasn't looking for love, but that might just be what found him—in the most interesting of ways.

Trigger Warnings: Violence, death, mentions of kidnapping, and other crimes against children.

CHAPTER ONE

Frankie

WE'D BEEN DRIVING for two days, and it felt like someone had replaced my eyelids with sandpaper. Technically, the drive should have only taken about three hours, but Gabe had been instructing me to drive in circles until I didn't even know which direction we were headed. Based on the position of the setting sun, we seemed to be headed in a generally north direction, but I couldn't even tell if we were still in Louisiana anymore, or if we had crossed into another state.

There would be some kind of toll or at least a sign if we crossed state lines, right?

That had been the case on every road trip I'd ever taken. Surely, I would know if we were in a different state.

I'd say Gabe was paranoid, if not for the fact that someone was actually trying to kill us.

Many someones, in fact. By that point, I'd lost track of who the most likely threat was supposed to be.

The mafia.

The secret pedophile ring.

The FBI.

Everyone was an enemy.

I shook my head, feeling the weight of my braids tickle against my neck. Rubbing my eyes to rid them of the sand building up in the corners, I focused back on the road.

We'd pulled off the main highway about fifteen minutes ago and were now traveling down a dirt road that seemed to be more dirt than road. I hesitated to even call it a road. It was more like a flat line between the trees where the roots didn't grow as thick.

Luckily, I'd had practice driving my parent's RV over some difficult terrain, because an inexperienced driver would have struggled to navigate the clunky vehicle between the trees.

To be fair, I struggled as well, but I'd kept the RV on all four wheels so far, so I considered it a success.

"Can't you drive more carefully," Newt complained from the back.

I gripped the steering wheel so tight I could feel the stitches in the leather. "You're lucky we're even staying upright. I'm not sure this is even a road."

I felt guilty the moment the words were out of my mouth. Newt was only worried for Sebastian, and to be honest, I was as well. The man was severely injured, and the constant jostling from the bumpy ride would only make it worse. Sebastian hadn't said a word in the last hour, yet I could feel the pain radiating from the back of the RV with every squeak of the vehicle's inadequate shocks.

"Hey, resting-blank-face, where are we going?"

Agent Gabe Long sat in the passenger seat next to me, staring ahead without a twitch of emotion on his face and his arms crossed over his chest.

I expected to be ignored, yet when I addressed him, he actually looked at me.

"Why do you insist on calling me these ridiculous names?"

I slowed the RV down to a crawl that barely registered on the speed dial as I eased the vehicle over a cluster of large tree roots. It was starting to rain, and I desperately wanted to get wherever we were going before a storm blew in and made the already difficult road even more treacherous.

To hide my nerves, I turned on a bright smile and grinned at the man sitting next to me. "Well, what else am I supposed to call you? You've never actually introduced yourself to me."

Finally, I'd earned some expression from the man. His brow furrowed as he thought back over the weeks we'd been forced to live together. I could tell the moment he realized I was speaking the truth, because his typically flat gaze sparked with a hint of life.

In the chaos of our first meeting, he'd never actually introduced himself.

"You know my name," he tried to argue.

I merely shook my head. "Knowing your name is not the same as being introduced. So, until you give me your name properly, I'll call you whatever I want."

We hit a flat patch of road and I dared to drive a little faster, almost hitting double digits on the speedometer.

The rain started falling harder, and ice crystallized around the edges of the windshield. It was going to be the most miserable kind of weather. Cold and wet. The kind of weather that hung right at the point of freezing without actually tipping over the edge, so everything turned into an ugly, muddy slush.

"I'm Agent Long," he said after several awkwardly silent moments with only the sound of the freezing rain on the metal roof to accompany us. "But just call me Gabe."

It was a pleasant surprise. I'd been expecting further arguments from the man and didn't even have to fake my smile.

"Glad to meet you, Gabe. I'd shake your hand, but I'm a little preoccupied at the moment."

That seemed to be as much heart-to-heart as Gabe could handle at once, because he merely nodded at a spot down the road to point out that our destination was coming up.

The road opened into a clearing in the trees, revealing a small house among the foliage. At the sight, I was equal parts relieved and annoyed. Relieved that we had finally reached the end of our journey, and annoyed that Gabe hadn't told me how close we were to the end sooner. The drive would have been a lot less stressful if I knew there were only a few minutes left.

I brought the RV to a stop right next to the front door, leaving just enough space for the motorized handicap lift. Getting Sebastian unloaded from the vehicle and inside the house was another ordeal. One that had us all grumbling in frustration, especially as the icy rain turned to sleet. The wheels of Sebastian's mobile bed stuck in the mud and wouldn't budge until both Gabe and Damien worked together to literally lift the entire thing.

However, after a lot of sweating and swearing, we were all safely inside. We were wet and cold, and probably looked like a pack of half-feral dogs, but we were unharmed.

Well, no more harmed than we had been when we started the journey. No one could look at Sebastian's state and call the man unharmed.

"Careful," I heard Newt say. "Try not to move around. I'm worried about that leg. It's been out of traction too long. If it starts healing the wrong way you may need more surgery to fix it, so keep your leg as still as possible until we get you set up."

Something warm, yet unsettled, squirmed in my chest. It was the same feeling that arose whenever one of my patients wasn't doing well. I hated that they were suffering, but I was glad I had the skills to do something about it.

No matter how tired I felt, and how much I just wanted to curl up on the first flat surface I could find and go to sleep, I couldn't rest until I knew everyone under my care was okay. Gathering my braids in my hands, I tied them back in a low ponytail to keep them out of my face. The familiar gesture acted like a trigger, putting me into *work mode.*

"Hey." I placed a hand on Newt's shoulder. "Come on. This place must have a bed somewhere. Let's get your man comfortable."

The bed that we'd stolen from the

hospital didn't want to roll over the house's carpet, especially not with mud clogging the wheels. Newt and I struggled to keep the bed moving without shoving it, but when I looked back at Gabe and Damien to ask for help, I found them engaged in an intense conversation.

It was probably a good idea to not interrupt men armed with guns, even if those guns were kept in hidden holsters under their jackets. Newt and I could take care of Sebastian on our own.

The house was small, so we didn't have to look very hard to find a bedroom. It was a room, with a bed, and that was it. There wasn't even a nightstand or a wardrobe to give the space a little character.

Between Newt's dual experience as a paramedic and a nurse, and my job as a physical therapist, we had plenty of practice on how to maneuver a patient. Yet, it still took all of our training to smoothly transfer Sebastian from the rolling hospital gurney to the proper bed.

I couldn't help but flinch. The man must be in so much pain, but he didn't make a sound. We'd given him as much pain medication as we'd dared, but drugs could only do so much.

From there, it became a flurry of activity as we got Sebastian's leg suspended back in its traction and checked his stitches and bandages. Everything seemed to still be in place, but only time would tell when it came to his internal injuries.

If the new pins in Sebastian's leg had shifted, or his broken ribs had been compromised, we likely wouldn't know until it was too late.

I tried not to think about it. There wasn't much we'd be able to do anyway, out in the middle of nowhere. This man needed to be in a hospital, but that wasn't possible right now, so Newt and I would just have to be good enough.

As soon as we got Sebastian secured in the bed, the man almost immediately fell asleep. It was no surprise. I felt ready to collapse myself. None of us had slept much over the last two days.

There wasn't anywhere to sit, so Newt and I turned the floor into our chair, with our backs against the wall and our shoulders leaning against each other.

"I can't believe it's been less than a week."

"Hmm?" I didn't remember closing my eyes but forced them open when I heard Newt's voice. "What do you mean?"

Newt wasn't looking at me. His gaze remained locked on his boyfriend.

"Less than a week ago we were celebrating the fact that Sebastian was finally up and walking unassisted. Now we're here. How did we even get here? It all seems like a blur."

He finally looked at me, tears making his blue eyes even bluer.

"I'm so sorry you got dragged into this, Frankie. You were just trying to help me and now I've ruined your life."

"Hey, hey, hey. None of that. You did not ruin my life." I bumped his shoulder with mine. "Although, I've definitely won the competition for 'Best Friend of the Decade'. I expect a medal. And a statue. A statue of me wearing a medal. Don't you think it would look really good standing right at the hospital entrance? Much better than that weird modern art... thing they commissioned last year."

Newt giggled. It was a tired but happy sound. Despite everything that had happened, his spirits weren't broken.

I breathed a sigh of relief. So long as

we still had the spirit to keep going, any problem could be solved eventually. I held tightly to that idea, no matter how unrealistic. It forced me out of bed on my worst days and helped me support the patients who were too exhausted to help themselves.

Newt and I talked for a while. So much had happened over the last few days, there hadn't been much time to just talk like we used to. We mostly stuck to shallow conversations that didn't require much thought. Rosalind, Newt's sister, was a popular topic. I'd never liked her patronizing attitude toward Newt. It seemed to come from a loving place, but good intentions didn't change how she always made Newt feel worse about himself.

Because of that, I regretted missing the moment she realized her assumptions about Sebastian had been wrong. I couldn't even imagine what her face must have looked like. The woman never admitted to any mistakes, and Newt's description just wasn't enough.

Maybe I could request the footage from the hospital security cameras. Such a sight needed to be seen with my own eyes, even if it was just on a grainy recording.

We talked so long that we eventually both ended up falling asleep on the floor, leaning against each other for support.

CHAPTER TWO

Frankie

I AWOKE TO the sound of arguing and instantly recognized both of the brothers' voices along with Gabe.

"Really, guys. Isn't there enough conflict in our lives already? Do you have to turn everything into a battle?"

I yawned so hard I feared my jaw would dislocate and scratched at my scalp. My braids felt dry and too loose at the root. They would have to be re-done soon.

"What are you even arguing about? Surely nothing bad has happened so soon. We just got here."

Three different sets of eyes turned toward me in unison. All of them dark. All of them angry. It would have been a terrifying sight to wake up to, except for the fact that they obviously weren't angry at me.

"Yeah, we just got here," Sebastian agreed with me, yet it sounded like he was saying something else.

Next to me, Newt stirred but didn't fully wake up. I moved his head off my shoulder and laid him flat on the floor. There was at least carpet, but it still didn't look very comfortable.

"Okay, what's going on?"

Sebastian, who was obviously still groggy and in pain from the pinched look on his face, glared at his brother. "Someone is being a hypocrite."

Damien sighed and ran a tired hand over his eyes. "I'm not being a hypocrite. It's a good idea and you know it."

"I know that for literal months you've been telling me to stay put. Stay inside. Don't go anywhere to do anything. But now that you're confined to one place, you can't even last a few hours before you're trying to leave."

I'd obviously slept through a

significant conversation, but there was no opportunity to ask as the brothers kept arguing.

"Sebastian, you had to stay in the apartment for the sake of your injuries. That has nothing to do with why I'm leaving now."

"Bullshit. Did you already forget how I got injured in the first place? There are people out there who tried to kill me. People who are just as much your enemies as mine. We fled to stay safe, again, so why are you trying to throw yourself right back into danger?"

Damien placed a hand on his brother's shoulder in what should have been a comforting gesture.

Sebastian tried to shove the other man away, but the sudden motion made him gasp with pain.

"Idiot, you need to calm down," Gabe scolded as he checked on Sebastian's injuries. He seemed to know exactly what to look for, indicating that Gabe probably had medical training.

It was a blatant reminder that I didn't really know anything about the man or his experiences before this whole fiasco.

Sebastian at least had enough

common sense not to try and smack Gabe away as well. Instead, he just stared stubbornly at the wall. "Sure. Calm down. Easy for you to say. It's not your family that's trying to get themselves killed."

Neither brother could see it since they weren't looking at Gabe, but I had a perfect view of the pained expression that flickered over his face.

It was brief. Almost as soon as the emotion came, Gabe schooled himself back into his usual stoicism.

"Damien isn't trying to get himself killed. He's doing this so you can both live."

Damien reached out like he was about to touch Sebastian again, but then changed his mind.

"We'll never be free until Russo and his entire empire falls. The FBI is cracking down harder on the Mariano family. Several of their warehouses have been raided and a few of their important allies have recently been arrested. This is our chance to make a definitive move against the man who killed our parents."

On the floor, Newt finally woke up. Blue eyes peeked out from under orange bangs and looked around with a puzzled expression.

"What's going on?" he asked me. Even though he was confused, he at least picked up on enough of the tension around us to realize that he should keep his voice to a whisper.

I also whispered back. "Sibling quarrel. I think it'll be over soon."

Sebastian no longer looked as angry as he had before. Now he was just resigned and sad. "Russo will never be stopped so long as he's got people within the FBI. Even getting him arrested wasn't enough. Nothing but death will ever stop that man."

Damien's answering smile was as sharp as the knife he probably had hidden away in his clothing somewhere. "That's why we need to take care of it ourselves. The FBI is just a distraction. I've got Mason and a few other people helping me, but I need to go back so we can keep pressing our advantage while we have it."

For a moment, Sebastian's dark gaze flicked in his brother's direction, but then immediately returned to his vigil of the wall. "Whatever. Don't know why you're bothering to tell me all this. You're going to do what you want anyway."

Sighing again, Damien grit his teeth like he was chewing on whatever he wanted to say, before turning to leave the room. He was almost out the door when Gabe grabbed his arm.

"Don't leave it like this."

Damien removed the other man's hand from his arm, but he stopped to listen to what Gabe had to say.

"What do you mean? Leave what like this?"

"Your brother. Don't leave with bad feelings between you. There's no guarantee when you'll see each other again."

It was the most I'd ever heard Gabe say at one time, and almost distracted me from the true meaning of his words.

When Damien left, there was no guarantee the brothers would *ever* see each other again.

With that painful reminder of our situation, Damien had no choice but to try and speak with his brother one more time. He stepped up beside the bed again, this time keeping his voice calm and choosing his words with care.

"Sebastian, I promise we will be free of

that monster someday, but that freedom won't come unless we find a way to take it for ourselves. For now, I need to leave, but I will come back. I always have, and I always will."

Sebastian's gaze hardened, like he was trying to hold onto his anger, but it didn't last. His face crumpled, and even though he was lying down, I could see the defeated slump to his shoulders.

"Yeah. I get it. Go save the day. I'll stay out of your way like a good little cripple."

"Hey, you aren't crippled." Damien raised his fist like he meant to punch Sebastian in the shoulder. It was a familiar show of affection I'd seen the brothers exchange before, but right now even such a simple gesture could be disastrous.

Newt and I both jumped up, ready to pull the man away before he could accidentally cause his brother more harm, but Gabe beat us to it. He grabbed Damien's wrist and forcibly lowered the man's fist with a shake of his head.

A look of sorrow twisted Damien's face when he realized his mistake.

Sebastian scoffed. "Not crippled? Right. Say that once I can walk again."

Standing tall and straightening his shoulders, Damien tugged the cuffs of his jacket back into place. "I will."

Sebastian scowled, but Damien only smiled.

"I'll say it again once you can walk." He looked over toward Newt and me. "With such a dedicated crew taking care of you, how can you expect anything other than a full recovery?"

Sebastian followed his brother's gaze, and his eyes softened the moment they landed on Newt.

I was happy for my friend. He deserved to have someone who looked at him with such obvious love, even if they hadn't said the words yet.

However, jealousy also gnawed at my heart. No one had ever looked at me that way. Not even my parents. They hadn't been abusive or neglectful, but they hadn't been very demonstrative in their affection either. A quiet nod or a quick word was usually all I got from them, and even that had stopped when I chose my college major.

Apparently physical therapist wasn't a glamorous enough career for them to acknowledge. They still seemed to think that this was some sort of weird hobby, and that I was just wasting time before eventually starting a *real* career.

This was not the time for such negative emotions. So, like usual, I folded them up and tucked them away in a far corner of my mind where they would remain forgotten.

A smile came to Sebastian's face. It was still strained, but at least he was putting in some effort to stay positive.

"Yeah. Don't take too long, Damien, or I'll be running circles around you when you come back."

When the brothers eventually parted a few minutes later, it was on much better terms. Newt stayed back with Sebastian, climbing into the bed beside him, but I followed Gabe and Damien out of the house.

The sleet had stopped for a moment, but the ground was still nothing but muddy slush. It was night, but even in the dark of the deep woods, I could tell how miserable the environment was.

I stayed safely on the front porch where the mud couldn't reach me.

The RV was still sitting by the front door, right where I'd parked it, and the sight of the vehicle reminded me of something.

"Wait. How are you leaving, Damien? Are you taking the RV?"

"No, you'll keep that in case Sebastian needs to be moved again. There's a town about ten miles away. I'll walk and find transportation there."

I scanned the dark trees again, then eyed Damien who was still dressed in the casual clothes and coat he'd been wearing when we made our quick escape from the hospital. His shoes at least looked sturdy, but the rest of his clothing didn't seem appropriate for the weather.

"You're going to hike ten miles through the woods? At night? In the rain?"

The sharp grin returned to his face. "I've made harder journeys. Take care of my brother. I'm counting on you and Newt to look after him."

Then, after adjusting his collar to shield his neck from the water dripping off the trees, Damien stepped off the porch and disappeared into the forest.

Gabe stood beside me as the two of us stared into the dark long after Damien had left.

"You have medical training, don't

you?" I said, just to break the silence. "I could tell from the way you looked over Sebastian's wounds."

In an oddly absent gesture, like he didn't even realize he was doing it, Gabe stroked a hand over his left arm. "I was a medic in the Army Rangers."

A normal person would have elaborated more, perhaps by describing what being a medic in the Army was like or what led him to such a position. However, Gabe was a man of few words. After speaking so much earlier, he was already beyond his normal limit.

A one sentence explanation was all I was going to get.

"Well, then I'll be relying on you along with Newt. We're going to need as much help as possible to get Sebastian back on his feet."

It was cold and my breath formed clouds in front of my face. I'd already started shivering just from standing outside for a few minutes.

How could Damien treat a ten mile hike in this weather like it was just a casual stroll?

I turned to go back inside where it was warm, but Gabe's voice stopped me.

"Do you really think he'll walk again?"

Images of Sebastian's x-rays and medical charts flashed through my mind. He'd been given a fifty percent chance of walking again, although after the difficult journey we'd put him through so soon after surgery, that number had probably lowered.

"That's up to him. All the medical care in the world won't matter if a patient doesn't put in the effort to get better."

Gabe stared back at the house like he could see Sebastian and Newt despite several closed doors standing between us and them.

"He'll get better. He's got too much to live for."

Remembering the warm look between Sebastian and Newt, and the obvious care the brothers had for each other even when fighting, I couldn't agree more.

Having reached my limit for cold temperatures, I trudged back inside. Newt was with Sebastian, so I didn't have to worry about my latest patient for the moment.

It was time to get some sleep. Dozing off while leaning against the wall had done nothing for my exhaustion, so I searched the house for an available bed.

Almost immediately, I found one.

Just one.

"Son of a bitch," I exclaimed. I searched the house again, just to make sure I hadn't missed a hidden door somewhere.

Nope. There was only one other bedroom, with only one bed.

Newt and Sebastian would be staying in the first bedroom, which meant Gabe and I would have to share the one remaining bed.

I'd already been sharing a bed with Gabe for weeks. Finally having my own place to sleep was the one thing I'd been looking forward to, but the house somehow seemed to be even smaller than Sebastian's apartment.

Maybe I could convince Gabe to sleep on the couch?

Checking the front room, the biggest couch I found was a loveseat meant for two. It would never fit a man of Gabe's height. I might be able to fit if I propped my feet up on the armrest, but that didn't sound very comfortable and there was no telling how long we'd be calling this place home.

Grumbling under my breath, I started collecting pillows and blankets to build a barrier wall down the center of the bed.

At least it was a queen-size bed so we wouldn't have to sleep on top of each other.

CHAPTER THREE

Gabe

GETTING SETTLED INTO the safe house took longer than I expected. Once we arrived, got Sebastian set up, and handled the argument around Damien leaving, I had hoped things would quiet down. But, no. We still needed supplies like food, clothes, and all the other odds and ends required for humans to live comfortably. Usually, a proper protection detail would already have this sorted out, but since we'd taken off without permission, the whole thing was a mess.

That is why I usually never acted without a clear plan. Plans kept things from getting messy.

There was no choice. As much as I hated leaving someone under my protection alone, I also didn't feel comfortable sending either Newt or Frankie into town by themselves. They were civilians. If they were attacked, they had no way to defend themselves.

There'd already been too many close calls under my watch. No more.

Unfortunately, I couldn't drive an RV—at least not confidently enough to be certain that I wouldn't tip the clunky thing—so Frankie had driven me into town and dropped me off at the nearest store, after which I'd ordered him to immediately drive back to the safe house. With a couple hours' effort, I managed to pick up all the supplies we'd need for at least a week, and also rented the most nondescript car I could find. The RV was necessary to safely transport Sebastian in his injured state, but it was too noticeable. We needed a better mode of transportation.

As soon as I returned to the safe house, I immediately locked myself in the bathroom.

There wasn't much privacy in a house

so small, and both bedrooms were occupied. Sebastian couldn't be moved, and I didn't have the heart to kick Frankie out of the little space he'd carved for himself. Sharing a bedroom with the man was hard enough without intentionally creating animosity between us.

The kitchen and front sitting room were also not private enough for my work, so the bathroom ended up becoming my office. Luckily the house had two bathrooms, so things wouldn't get messy.

Why was everything always a mess?

I perched on the edge of the tub, looking over the files I had stacked on the floor and the laptop that sat open on the sink counter.

Sebastian and Damien were so focused on Russo and the Mariano family, they refused to hear about anything else. However, I had my doubts about their involvement with the pedophile ring. So far, the only connection that we had found between the Mariano family and the pedophile ring was Lorenz Mariano, Russo's brother-in-law. The man was certainly scum, but he wasn't 'ring leader' material either.

No. Lorenz Mariano was certainly

funding this pedophile ring, probably to supply his own desires, but he wasn't the one pulling the strings. Someone else was in charge of this little ring of bottom feeders. Someone powerful enough to accept funding from the Mariano family without crumbling under the pressure of such a dangerous debt.

I wouldn't be able to conduct this investigation on my own. Especially not with the limited resources I currently had. I would need help.

My fingers flew over the keys of my laptop, bringing up a video call with a familiar number.

It picked up almost immediately.

"Gabe. I wondered when you'd be calling me."

Lily Kim's smiling face greeted me through the screen.

"It's a bad situation. Not many people I can trust right now."

As the FBI director's personal secretary, Lily was one of the few people not afraid of the man. According to her, it was hard to be afraid of someone when you knew their every coming and going. She probably knew more about the director's life than even he did. Someone like David Russo would commit genocide to get someone like her on his payroll. The information she knew could topple whole countries.

She was also one of the few people I trusted to help me, even if it meant acting against her own boss.

"This is a secure line, right?" she asked even as her fingers typed at her computer to double check.

I just gave her a look, knowing that would be enough to get my message across.

"Right, right," she waved me off with one hand even as her other kept typing. "This isn't your first rodeo. You know what you're doing."

Her long black hair was twisted up around a jade hair stick that was carved into the shape of a lily, just like her name. Her whole desk had a generally floral theme, from her stationery to the earrings dangling off her ears. It tended to give people the wrong impression of her, that she was some delicate blossom who would wilt at the slightest pressure.

Nothing could be further from the truth.

I'd seen her kill a man with that exact

same hair stick before.

"So, Gabe. You're certainly in deep this time. These brothers must have gotten under your skin if you're going this far to protect them."

The woman was far too perceptive. It was a blessing when used to my advantage, but a curse when used against me.

Yes, the Roth brothers had struck a chord with me from the minute I'd first heard their story. Successfully dodging both the mafia and witness protection when they were barely just adults was an impressive feat, and a shame that it was even needed. Witness protection should have lived up to its name and protected them.

Just like it should have done this time. I shouldn't need to run away from my own organization just to keep innocent people safe.

Plus, Sebastian's relationship with the little nurse was so sweet it practically demanded protection.

Then there was the other man. Frankie... I still didn't know what to think of him, but he had given up everything to help his friend without hesitation, and that was an admirable trait.

Overall, they were a group of people worth protecting, and there weren't nearly enough people trying to protect them.

"Hmmm," Lily grinned at me as she tapped a pen against her desk. "You've got your thinking face on. Something interesting about your little lost lambs that you'd like to share?"

"No. And I'm not telling you where I've taken them."

"Probably one of the safe houses, I'm assuming, though I won't bother asking which one. So, what do you need from me?"

Sighing deeply, I leaned back and pinched the bridge of my nose, nearly falling over when I forgot that I was sitting on the edge of the tub and not a chair.

"Right now, I'm acting outside of orders. This would be so much easier if it was a sanctioned mission."

"So, I'm guessing you want to schedule a meeting with the director. See if you can get things sorted with him after your little runaway act." She started scribbling something down in her day planner, which was also decorated in a colorful flower theme.

"Face to face would be best. At a neutral location. I don't think the director is our enemy, but I also don't want him to know where the Roth brothers are until I'm certain that he's on our side."

Or that Damien Roth had already run off on his own to continue waging his one-man war against David Russo.

"Neutral location," Lily nodded. "Already ahead of you. Got the perfect place in mind, and I should be able to open a spot in the director's schedule in two days. Think you can wait until then?"

"It'll have to do. Anything on your end you think I should know about?"

She finished writing and set the day planner back in its designated place on her desk. It was one of the reasons she and I got along so well. We both hated mess.

She then pulled out two files from somewhere beyond the camera's view and held them up so I could see their identical blank covers.

"I've got two things for you. Which would you like first?"

CHAPTER FOUR

Gabe

COFFEE SHOPS WERE usually places I avoided as much as possible. So many different smells in the air, plus the noise of people talking and coffee beans grinding, made for an overwhelming mix of sensations.

However, the coffee shop I found myself in less than a day after talking with Lily was connected to a bookshop, so it wasn't too bad. Most people were sitting around reading a book rather than talking, and those who did engage in conversation kept their voices at a minimum level. The coffee grinder was even isolated in a back room so it didn't disturb the atmosphere.

It was a place I would have enjoyed spending some time if I wasn't in a hurry. The drive here from the safe house had taken several hours, and I didn't want to leave the others alone any longer than necessary.

If someone managed to find the safe house when I wasn't there...

It wasn't even worth thinking about. They would be fine. I'd done everything I could to cover our tracks and make sure no one had followed us or knew where we were.

Yet, the gruesome images wouldn't leave my mind.

Sebastian gunned down in his sickbed.

Newt crumpled in a heap on the floor with his blood staining the carpet.

Frankie beaten to death as he tried to defend his friends, because there was no way the man would go down without a fight.

No, it wasn't worth thinking about, because it wouldn't happen. I would finish my business and return to a house filled with three perfectly safe and bored individuals.

GABE

"Agent Long?" a small voice asked from behind me.

I controlled the urge to flinch, uncomfortable with having anyone standing out of sight at my back. Setting down the book I'd been reading—it wasn't as good as the cover had promised—I rose from the table and turned to meet the newcomer.

A woman stood just a few feet away, looking small and nervous.

"Miss Bell, I assume."

"Yes, um, that's me."

She wrung her hands before tucking them into the front pockets of her overalls. They were stained and frayed in a few places, but obviously well loved and cared for. Along with the two thick braids that hung over her shoulders and her heart shaped face, she looked like a modern Dorothy Gale. I could easily picture her working on a Kansas farm and singing about rainbows.

When she didn't move or say anything else, I gestured for her to take the seat across the table from me.

"Now, Miss Bell, I've looked over the information you gave the agency."

"Oh, call me Tansie. Miss Bell sounds

so formal."

"Okay Miss... Tansie. I'll get right to the point. You claim to have found your son."

Her hands started fidgeting again, this time toying with something in her pocket. "Well, I didn't exactly find him. That's actually the problem. I can't find him."

Her words came out in a rush, tripping over each other so I could barely understand what she was saying.

"Take a deep breath and tell me everything from the beginning."

She ended up taking several breaths before she could continue. I tapped my foot impatiently against the bag sitting on the floor beside my chair as I waited.

If anyone asked, I'd only bought the books in order to avoid looking suspicious as I hung around the bookstore, but that would be a lie. I'd bought them for myself. There was no telling how long I was going to be stuck playing bodyguard for Sebastian and the others. I would need something to keep my mind distracted, and books usually did the trick.

Eventually, the woman collected her nerves enough to speak straight.

"A few years ago I, um... I gave birth to

a child. I was young. Barely out of high school. I couldn't look after a kid, so I gave him up."

She hesitated again, probably waiting for me to cast judgment on her for her life choices. It was none of my business, and I honestly didn't care that she'd had a child so young out of wedlock. The only thing that mattered to me was getting the info I needed as soon as possible.

"All right." I nodded and tried to hurry her along. "Since you claim you found your child, I assume you eventually went looking for him."

"Well, no. I didn't go looking. I ran into him by accident."

She pulled out her phone and showed me a photo. It was blurry around the edges and sat at an awkward angle, but a young boy stood out prominently at the center of the image. He looked to be maybe eight years old and bore almost no resemblance to the woman sitting across from me.

"And you're certain this child is yours because..." I trailed off, letting her fill in the rest of the question on her own.

"I knew the boy's father practically since we were born. You know the old story. Grew up as neighbors. High school sweethearts. Broke up when we went to college. The whole thing. And this boy…" She tapped the picture, accidentally zooming in on the kid's face. "This boy is the spitting image of my ex at that age. I passed him on the street one day and I just knew. For years, I'd wondered what happened to him, and seeing him in person, I got curious. It was a closed adoption, so I hired an investigator to look into it for me. But the investigator found nothing. There's no record I even gave birth. I kept looking, but no matter what I did, I kept hitting a dead end. According to the law, my son doesn't exist. But I know he exists. I gave birth to him. That's not something you just forget about."

The pocket of her overalls was deeper than expected, and she pulled out a folder containing several pages of notes.

"This is everything I've been able to find, and also everything I remember about my son. Please. I'm not looking to take him back, especially if he's in a good home. But I just want to make sure he's okay."

Taking the pages from her, I quickly scanned over the information.

GABE

I found what I was looking for right on the first page. The hospital where she'd given birth was already on our watch list. Several other children had gone missing from there. Tansie Bell and her son were just more victims to add to the list.

One more piece of evidence added to an ever-growing pile.

"There have been several other instances of parents like you, who surrendered their children for adoption only for the records of the child to disappear. We're already looking into it. But thank you for bringing this to us. Is there anything else you can remember about the boy you saw? Something that might help us locate him."

She thought it over for a second as her hands nervously tugged at one of her braids.

"I'm not sure. I was in such shock at the time, I barely managed to snap that single picture. He was with an adult, but I don't remember much about them. I wrote down the exact location where I saw him. Will that help?"

Flipping through the pages, I found the correct information. It was extremely precise, not only listing the exact location, but also the date and time down to the minute. If there were any security cameras in the area, I'd definitely be able to find the right footage.

This might all be a wild goose chase. The kid might not even be hers, but her story aligned too well with the other missing kids Sebastian had discovered. That wasn't something I could just ignore.

"Thank you, miss. I'll look into it and let you know what I find."

I gave her a number where she could safely reach me before grabbing my bag of books and standing from the table to leave. It was perhaps rude to make my exit so quickly, but I was on a time crunch and couldn't waste time catering to social obligations.

As I turned to go, the woman stopped me.

"Agent... um, Agent Long. What do you think happened with my son? Is he okay? He's not in any sort of danger, is he?"

Once upon a time, years ago, lying had been difficult for me. As a child, I'd been honest to the point of being brutal and it lost me many friends.

Now, I barely flinched as the words left my mouth.

"I'm sure everything is fine. It's probably just a bureaucratic error that needs to be fixed."

She breathed an audible sigh of relief. "Oh, that's good. When I realized there was no record of him, I thought something terrible must have happened. It shouldn't be so easy for children to just disappear."

"No," I wholeheartedly agreed. "No, it shouldn't be so easy for children to disappear."

CHAPTER FIVE

Gabe

AFTER THE MEETING with Miss Tansie Bell, I wanted to immediately drive back to the safe house to check on everyone. However, I wasn't done for the day.

Instead of returning to the safe house, I drove forty more minutes in the opposite direction, putting an even greater space between me and the people I needed to protect. It aggravated every nerve I had and tested my patience to its limit. I was left feeling more and more agitated with every mile that passed beneath the tires of my car, but it was necessary. Lily had given me two items of business to take care of, and I wanted to get them both out of the way before I met with the director tomorrow.

As I stood in the foyer of an empty apartment, listening for the sound of footsteps outside the door, I began to question that decision. Surely there were better things I could be doing with my time than standing around in the dark like an obsessive stalker.

What was taking the man so long?

According to his daily schedule, he usually arrived home about half an hour ago. Of all the days for this man to get delayed, it had to be the exact moment when I was waiting for him.

Nearly twenty more minutes of waiting finally paid off when the front door swung open on squeaky hinges.

I stood as still as possible.

The familiar figure of Blake Adder, my fellow agent who had worked with me on many cases, walked past. It was his own apartment, so he easily navigated the room using only the miniscule light that snuck around the edges of the closed curtains.

Just as he reached the far side of the room, I flicked the switch on the wall.

GABE

The room filled with light. He jumped, nearly tripping over the coffee table as he reached for his gun.

Upon seeing me standing in a hidden corner by the front door, he pressed a hand against his chest and gasped.

"Jesus, Gabe. Don't do that. I nearly shot you."

"I've seen you during training. Your trigger control is better than that."

"Well, you nearly gave me a heart attack."

I stepped further into the room and took a seat on one of the two chairs facing each other. The white leather furniture looked much better than it felt. Blake had a pretentious taste in decoration that I had never understood.

"Are you saying you weren't expecting me to show up?"

He claimed the other chair, gun still clutched in his hand though it hung limp and remained pointed at the ground.

"Yeah, I did, but not like this. How'd you even get in here anyway?"

I raised one eyebrow, waiting to see if he actually needed me to answer that question.

He didn't.

"Right, why am I asking?" He ran an exasperated hand through his hair and stored his gun back in its holster. "Fuck. What kind of skills did they teach you in the army? I can't that imagine lock picking is a part of the standard training regime."

"Not standard. No."

Then again, nothing about the Army Rangers was ever standard. It was about getting the job done however possible, and with whatever skills were needed.

Didn't have the skills needed?

Then you either learned quick or you died.

The ability to pick a lock had saved my life on more than one occasion.

"Well..." Blake leaned back in his chair. "Now that you've made your entrance. What do you want? You know the director is still steaming mad about the stunt you pulled. Seriously. I think there was literal steam coming out of his ears at one point."

I tugged at the sleeves of my jacket, undoing the cufflinks to give my wrists a little more breathing room. "I've made an appointment to talk with him tomorrow. For now, you're my main concern. You were put in charge of investigating the explosion at the Roth Brothers' apartment. What have you found?"

Blake hid his face in his hands for a moment as he mumbled to himself, likely wondering how he always ended up in these situations.

To be fair, the man did have an uncanny ability for ending up as the middleman in a lot of investigations. Always in the middle of things, but never actually in charge.

"Fine," he eventually concluded. "This is priority information, but whatever. You're still an agent, so you still have clearance. Let them try to fire me. See what happens."

He stood and retrieved a file from somewhere in another room. When he returned, he set the file down on the table in front of me.

I immediately started going through the information as he sat back in his chair and gave me a basic summary.

"It's as we expected. A bomb was wired into the door, which was triggered when Sebastian Roth opened it. Nasty piece of work, too. There was an incendiary device added to the bomb specifically designed to spread as much fire as possible, which is why the apartment burned so quickly. They really wanted to make sure your man was dead. If the initial explosion didn't kill him, the ensuing fire would."

"But they failed. He survived."

"Yeah. Those Roth brothers must be made of something special, because honestly, I have no idea how he survived."

At the back of the file, I found a page with several photos attached, including one that looked like a pile of broken bricks. "Sebastian and Damien Roth have had to fight for their survival since they were little more than teenagers. To have lasted this long, it should be no surprise that they're good at surviving. But that's not what I want to know about. The nature of the bomb doesn't surprise me. Its placement, however, is a concern. How was it planted inside the apartment when we had the building secured? I was guarding the place myself. No outsider should have been able to get in."

Between my meeting with Tansie Bell, and now with Blake Adder, I'd been talking a lot that day. My throat was starting to feel raw, but there was no chance to let it rest. My meeting with the director tomorrow would require just as much talking as today. Possibly even more.

All I could do was keep pushing forward and hope my voice didn't give out.

Blake gestured toward the file in my hand. "I found the answer to that. It's documented on the last page. There was a maintenance shaft in the basement that we missed. It wasn't secure. That seems to be how the person who planted the bomb got into the building. Once inside, it wouldn't be hard to sneak up to the Roth apartment. And you've already demonstrated how easy it is to pick a lock."

I looked back at the page in question, which was already sitting open in my hand. Just as Blake had described, it showed several pictures of a basement, including a close up of the hatch to the maintenance shaft.

"Where's agent Wilson?"

Blake was obviously surprised by the sudden change of topic and took several moments to respond to what should have been an easy question. "What?"

"Agent Gloria Wilson," I snapped, already getting impatient. "She was working this case with you, wasn't she?"

"Oh, right. She's been out sick with pneumonia. The weather's been terrible recently and I guess it got to her."

Remembering the frozen sleet that had greeted our arrival at the safe house and made transferring Sebastian out of the RV infinitely harder, I could agree with at least one thing he said.

"A lot of things have been terrible recently." I held up the pictures of the basement. "You know, we didn't miss this maintenance shaft. We discounted it because it was bricked over when the building was renovated. To get in that way, the wall would first have to be demolished."

"Yes," Blake agreed with me, though he elongated the word like he wasn't sure what to do with it. "Which you can clearly see in that picture. Someone broke through the wall from the outside."

"It is very clear in the picture," I agreed. "Except... Did you know I was recently able to get a look at Agent Wilson's original notes. She wrote down that the basement was the only part of the building to remain untouched by fire or explosion. She even included her own pictures with the note. Although, in her pictures this wall was clearly still intact."

I held up the picture of the broken bricks so both of us could see it.

"Strange how the wall wasn't broken until after Agent Wilson went on sick leave."

The two of us stared at each other, neither speaking. We didn't even blink. No more words were necessary. My meaning was clear.

A deep rumble, almost like a growl, built in the back of Blake's throat and his fingers slowly curled into fists. "Where did you see Wilson's original file?"

That answer didn't require words either, which was good, because I was running out.

He answered it for me.

"It was that Chinese cunt, wasn't it? Should have dealt with her when I had the chance."

Although I didn't react outwardly, internally I laughed at the idea of Blake ever having a chance to *deal* with Lily.

I set the file back on the table between us and tugged at the cuff of my left sleeve again.

"First, Lily is Korean. Not Chinese. If

you're going to insult someone, at least be accurate. And second..."

Between one word and the next, I pulled out a knife that was strapped to the inside of my wrist and threw it at Blake. The four-inch-long blade planted deep in his gut before he even realized what was happening.

"Wha—"

He never got to finish his question as the pain hit. His hand pressed against his stomach, and he seemed genuinely shocked to find it covered in blood.

The poor white furniture was going to be ruined.

"Don't move around too much," I said as I stood from my own spotless chair. "Gut wounds are tricky. They bleed slow, so you should survive."

He tried to stand and face me, but the pain knocked him off his feet and he slid to his knees. The hand not pressing against his stomach moved toward his gun, but I grabbed the weapon out of its holster before he had a chance.

"I told you not to move around too much."

The blood was coming faster now, staining the whole front of his body a deep crimson, like someone had poured paint on him.

Luckily, I'd brought a few first aid supplies, just in case.

I helped Blake lie on the floor, then started wrapping bandages and tape around the wound while keeping the knife in place.

"You just stabbed me. Why're you helping me?"

"I didn't stab you. I threw the knife at you."

He snorted in frustration, and I was happy to hear his lungs were clear. That meant the internal damage wasn't too bad.

"Whatever. Same thing. Why're you helping me?"

Once certain he wasn't about to bleed out on the floor, I pulled out my own gun and pressed the barrel against his temple.

"Because we aren't done. How long have you been working for the Mariano family? Did they get to you at some point, or have you been rotten from the start."

"Fuck off," he spat.

I pressed the gun in a little harder, enough to feel the flesh and bone of his temple grind against the metal. "Answer me and I'll let you crawl back to your masters. Keep quiet and I'll ship you back to them in multiple boxes."

He glared at me in silence.

Breathing deeply through my nose, I swung my gun to the side and pulled the trigger, shooting him in the knee.

A tangled knot of curses fell from Blake's lips as he tried to grab his knee, but the knife in his gut kept him from curling up.

"Stop moving around." I shoved him onto his back, then started bandaging this new wound.

The knee was completely demolished, and I felt a bit of satisfaction when I realized it was the right knee. The same leg that Sebastian currently had hanging in traction.

Now Sebastian wasn't the only one who may never walk again.

"You fucking psycho," Blake shouted, but there was a new fear in his eyes that hadn't been there before.

"It doesn't really matter how long you've been working for them," I said, as if he hadn't just insulted me. "Betrayal is still betrayal. What I really want to know is the identity of the person leading the pedophile ring Sebastian was investigating."

Blake's expression changed from one of fear and anger to one of confusion.

I shrugged, treating his confusion the same way one would treat a college student that couldn't recite their ABCs.

"What? I know Lorenz Mariano is bankrolling this secret ring, and the Mariano family is assisting in the hunt for Sebastian because of their own history with the brothers, but they aren't the ones in charge of the ring. Someone else is. That's the person I want."

I'd made a mistake. Asking such an unexpected question had shocked Blake, which distracted him from his fear. My desire to return to the safe house as soon as possible had caused me to rush things, and now I could already see the defiance building in Blake's eyes again.

Acting quickly, I pulled the knife out of his gut. My first aid attempts were ruined, and a fresh wave of blood gushed from the wound.

"You—"

He shut up real quick when I pointed the tip of the knife at his already destroyed knee, but I didn't want silence.

I wanted him talking.

He still wasn't afraid enough yet.

I let the point of the knife drag up his leg, keeping my gaze locked on his eyes to catch even the slightest change in expression.

The knife pointed at his groin.

There. Now he was afraid.

I pressed the knife down a little more, just enough for the tip to poke through the material of his pants and prick at his skin.

"All right. I'll tell you. Stop."

The knife stayed in place, but I didn't push it any farther.

"The person in charge of the pedophile ring," I demanded. "Not just their name. Tell me everything you know about them."

Blake's grin verged on mania. "I'll do you one better. Inside my safe, I've got several files of information on the whole nasty little undertaking. You can have it. But you're not going to like what you find."

I removed the knife, and re-bandaged his stomach. There was now a worrying amount of blood staining the floor around him. The man would need to get to a proper hospital soon if he was going to survive.

Before leaving, I'd have to make sure to call 911 for him. With this much blood loss, he might pass out before he could do it himself. I'd killed people before. Between my time in the Army Rangers, and my employment with the FBI, taking a life was nothing new. However, I refused to kill when it wasn't strictly necessary. It felt like a waste, and waste was almost synonymous with mess.

I really hated when things got messy.

Once certain that he wasn't about to die, I turned my attention to the safe in his closet. To my surprise, the door opened on the first try. I'd half expected him to give me a false code or try to lead me into a trap.

Apparently threatening to cut off a man's genitalia was enough to keep him honest. It was too bad Blake hadn't had someone holding a knife to his balls all his life. He'd be the saintliest man alive today, and then maybe we could have avoided this whole mess.

The safe was mostly empty except for a small stack of files at the very bottom. I pulled them out and flipped the top one open to the first page.

After such a long day dealing with people, my vocal cords were exhausted, and I had very few words left.

In fact, I had only one word left, which I shouted as soon as I saw what the file contained.

"Fuck."

CHAPTER SIX

Frankie

I HEARD THE crash all the way in the kitchen where I was making lunch. Granted, the safe house wasn't very big, but it was surprisingly well insulated. Sound didn't travel very far when the doors were closed, so the fact that I could hear the noise from several rooms away meant it must have been loud.

Taking just long enough to safely store the sharp kitchen knife away, I ran to the back bedroom. Not sure what I would find on the other side, I turned the knob and opened the door carefully. Sebastian lay sprawled on the floor, still tangled in the bed sheets, with Newt flittering around like a distressed hummingbird.

"Oh my God. Are you okay? No, of course you're not. Don't move. What hurts?"

I grabbed my friend and stopped him from tripping over his own boyfriend.

"What happened?"

Newt knelt on the floor next to Sebastian and checked the man for a concussion. "Well, I guess Sebastian tried to lean too far over the edge of the bed. I only looked away for a moment, but it was my fault. I should have been paying more attention."

"Ugh, stop it." Sebastian batted Newt's hand away. "It's not... I was just trying to reach the glass on the table. I should at least be able to get my own damn drink of water."

While Newt helped Sebastian to sit up, I found the glass in question. It was lying on the floor, its contents now soaking into the carpet. Based on the water ring on the table, however, the glass had previously been just a little too far away for Sebastian to reach. Instead of asking for help, the idiot had tried to get it himself.

As much as I loved my job as a

physical therapist, this was one of the things I hated about working with patients. They could be so stubborn, even to their own detriment.

Unfortunately, Gabe wasn't available to help. He'd left to go meet with some people and hadn't said when he'd be back. So, Newt and I had no choice but to hoist Sebastian back into the bed by ourselves.

As the taller of the two of us, I took Sebastian's upper body and hooked my arms under his shoulders. Newt took charge of Sebastian's legs, being very careful of his cast. Together, the two of us managed to lift the larger man. It wasn't graceful, and the movement jostled Sebastian around more than I would've liked, but it worked.

Once Sebastian was settled, I reached for the pillows to rearrange them, only to find a red smear of blood staining my skin. I stared at it for a moment, wondering how I'd hurt myself. Then the truth hit me.

The blood wasn't mine.

I glanced back at Sebastian, noting the man had a grimace on his face. He knew what I'd just realized.

"Show me."

For a moment it looked like he would argue, but then he sighed and gave in. Lifting up his shirt, he showed me his ribs. A few had been cracked in the explosion back at the apartment, and large ugly bruises ran up and down his side. There were even deep gashes where something had raked against his ribs. The damage had been fixed up in the hospital, but his tumble had ripped a few of the stitches. Some of the dark strings hung loose, and blood seeped freely from the wound.

The bleeding was sluggish, so it wasn't an immediate danger, but would need to be repaired right away.

"Uh, Newt, we've got a problem."

"I'll say."

I met Newt's eye to find him holding a metal pole.

When Sebastian fell off the bed, he'd knocked his traction rigging over as well, which had made most of the crashing sound I heard. The fall had damaged the rigging, and even from a quick observation I could tell it wasn't salvageable. It would need to be replaced.

Re-stitching some wounds we could

handle, but replacing the traction rigging would be a much harder problem to solve.

"Damn it," I grumbled as I cleaned the blood from my hands. "Perfect time for Gabe to be gone. We don't have a way to fix this."

"We might be able to rig something up with what we have here," Newt suggested. "Maybe tie some towels between a few chairs." He was already grabbing the nearest chair and lining it up with the bed. It wasn't tall enough. If we stacked the chair on top of something else it might work, but such a structure would be unstable at best and a hazard at worst.

I huffed and ran a hand through my braids.

"That might work temporarily, but I wouldn't trust it long term."

I sighed again, then stood up straight with a new facade of confidence.

"All right, here's what we're going to do. Newt, get your man stitched up and check to see if he has any other wounds he hasn't told us about." I glared at Sebastian, and the man at least had enough sense to look abashed over his actions. "Meanwhile, I'll drive into town and see what I can find to build a new traction frame. We've still got the RV. It's not the most efficient vehicle, but it'll get me there and back."

I headed for the door, eager to take action.

Newt followed me.

"But, Frankie, Gabe said not to use our credit cards since they can be tracked. How will you buy anything?"

That was a good point. I stopped in my tracks halfway to the door.

"I think Gabe left behind some emergency cash. Let me check."

I ended up having to search through the FBI Agent's stuff in the bedroom before eventually finding an envelope with some cash tucked away in a folder. Most of the cash I left alone, only taking as much as I thought I would need, but I still felt guilty. Technically, it wasn't my money, so this could be called stealing.

No, it was supposed to be for emergencies, and this counted as an emergency. We were left alone, and Sebastian needed something to help with his healing. Besides, Gabe and I were sharing the bedroom. In such a setup, he couldn't expect privacy.

I certainly didn't have any.

After giving Newt one final reassurance that I would be back soon, and reminding him to keep the doors locked, I hopped into the RV.

Maneuvering the cumbersome vehicle was easier this time since it wasn't raining and I actually knew where I was going. Still, the ten-mile drive into town took me nearly half an hour to navigate. Then there was another twenty minutes of aimless driving before I found a hardware store. The town didn't have much, but I couldn't help looking around with suspicious eyes.

Was that person walking on the sidewalk staring at the RV with too much interest?

Was the car behind me on the road following me?

Someone outside the hardware store was talking on the phone.

Who were they calling?

Were they reporting me to someone?

After pulling the RV into a parking spot, I took a deep breath and leaned my head against the steering wheel. Spending so much time with Gabe was making me paranoid. Yes, people were out to get us, but that didn't mean the whole world was our enemy.

The hardware store ended up being one of those mom and pop places where everything is organized in a way that only makes sense to the owner. I searched the shelves for a few minutes on my own but ended up having to ask the person working there for help. I gave a vague description of what I was trying to make, without revealing what it was for, and they helped me find the materials I would need. They even gave me a few ideas about how to make the whole structure sturdier, just in case Sebastian got the urge to be self-sufficient and fell out of bed again.

Hopefully, that wouldn't happen. His wounds didn't need any more stress, but I would rather be overly prepared than taken by surprise.

By the time I left the hardware store, I'd already been away from the safe house for an hour and a half. Newt would be worried, and there would be hell to pay if Gabe came back while I was gone. I should have immediately returned to the safe house, but my eye caught on the grocery store standing next to the hardware store.

GABE

Gabe had bought us basic supplies already, but the man seemed to be under the impression that living like he was still in the army was acceptable, and that everyone would be happy with such conditions. Protein drinks and granola bars were okay for a few meals, but we were going to need some more variety in our diets if we were going to be living there for a while.

Not to mention a few creature comforts would be nice. The man hadn't even bought us shampoo. Just plain bars of soap.

I scratched at my braids, which were in desperate need of some attention.

Yeah, there was no argument. I was definitely getting a few extra things at the store.

Another half hour later, and with the cash I'd brought nearly depleted, I was ready to return to the safe house. Only a little daylight remained, so I hurried back. Driving through the woods in the dark had been difficult enough the first time. I didn't want to do it again.

The last rays of sunlight were just fading to twilight among the forest's canopy when I pulled the RV up to the safe house.

"Oh, shit."

All my rushing to get back to the safe house had been pointless. Another car already sat in the clearing.

Gabe had returned before me.

Breathing deeply through my nose in an effort to rally my patience—the kind I usually reserved only for the most difficult patients—I braced myself to enter the house.

There were too many bags for me to carry in one go, so I started with the grocery items. A few of my purchases were perishable, so I wanted to get them in the refrigerator right away.

I managed to get all the way to the kitchen and set the bags down on the table before I was noticed.

"Where have you been?"

I held a sigh back behind my teeth at the sound of Gabe's demand.

"I just went out to get some things," I said as I started storing the items away in the mostly empty cabinets. "We needed—"

"I can see what you needed."

Gabe held up the bag of M&Ms I'd bought for Newt. They were his favorite, and my friend had been so stressed trying to take care of Sebastian. A little chocolate was usually the quickest way to calm him down. Yet, Gabe stared at me with a judgmental eye, as if I'd brought cocaine into the house.

Breathe, I reminded myself. It was no different than dealing with a headstrong patient that questioned all of my instructions.

Just breathe.

"You weren't here, and Sebastian needed a few things, so I went out. Nothing happened, and everything is fine. There's no reason to get mad."

Although I hadn't finished putting everything away, I left the kitchen and headed back out to the RV to fetch the supplies from the hardware store. I had at least put away the perishables. Everything else could sit on the kitchen table until later. I refused to stand around and be scolded like a child.

Unfortunately, Gabe was insistent on making his opinions known and followed me out to the RV.

"What if something had happened to you while you were alone? Or what if something had happened here?"

Grabbing the last of the bags out of the

RV, I slammed the door hard enough that the window seemed in danger of breaking.

"It was fine. Newt was here with Sebastian. I told them to keep the doors locked. They survived just fine without me for a little while."

I was on the front porch, almost back inside the house, when Gabe's words stopped me in my tracks.

"I'm almost not surprised by your disregard for your own safety, but I thought you'd at least show more care for your patient."

"What?" My footsteps echoed on the wooden boards of the porch as I turned around slowly to face the man standing just a few feet away. "What the hell is that supposed to mean?"

Gabe crossed his arms over his chest, making him look even larger. Although I stood on the porch and his feet were planted on the ground, he barely had to look up to meet my eye.

"You promised to help Sebastian recover. You're a physical therapist. It's your job to help take care of people. Yet, you left the people relying on you alone and vulnerable so you could go shopping for junk. If you're this irresponsible with all your patients, then healthcare probably isn't the best career for you."

We hadn't known each other very long. Only a few weeks. Yet, somehow, Gabe knew exactly how to hit me where it hurt most. A literal stab to the chest would have been less painful. My job was one of the most important things in my life. Some days it felt like the only thing keeping me going. To say I didn't deserve my job was basically the same as saying I didn't deserve life.

He said it so matter-of-factly as well. I would have preferred if he screamed or got mad. Then I could excuse his statement as a fit of emotion.

But no.

He spoke calmly and disregarded my life's work as if it were an obvious fact.

I stood frozen on the porch. A cool wind blew through the trees now that the sun had set, and goosebumps prickled my skin. Yet, I couldn't even bring myself to move two steps into the warmth of the house.

"Hey, Frankie, you're back," Newt's voice greeted me and broke the silence.

I turned away from Gabe and found my friend standing in the open doorway.

The light from inside the house glowed at his back.

"Did you get the stuff? You were right. My idea with the chairs isn't going to last. It's almost fallen over twice now. I hope you were able to find something."

He was smiling, but the expression didn't reach his eyes. I'd known the man long enough to recognize what was going through his head. He'd heard my argument with Gabe and was coming to my rescue.

The relief that filled my chest was so strong I nearly kissed him. Instead, I held up the bags still clutched in my hands. "Yep. Got it. The person at the hardware store gave me some ideas, too, so we should be able to come up with something."

"Great." Newt grabbed my arm and pulled me inside. "Come on. Sebastian is asleep right now, so it's perfect timing. If we have to move him again it won't cause him any pain."

We brought the bags into the far bedroom where, just as Newt had said, Sebastian was deeply asleep. He was still on a lot of painkillers, and I was honestly surprised he managed to stay awake as often as he did.

We dumped the contents of the hardware store bags onto the floor and started sorting through the different bits and pieces. Thanks to the instructions I'd gotten at the store, it wasn't hard to come up with a viable idea to replace the broken traction frame. The two of us sat on the floor like children putting together a puzzle. Through our efforts, little by little, the contraption started to take shape.

I was in the middle of struggling with a difficult screw that didn't want to fit into place when Newt suddenly spoke up.

"I noticed you got some other stuff."

"Yeah," I said without looking up. The screw had just started to behave, and I didn't want to let it get away from me. "Just some food and basic stuff, you know. To make living here a little more comfortable."

"Great. I'm starving, and Sebastian is going to need plenty of good nutrition while he's healing."

The screw finally fell into place, and I laughed. "You and your freak of nature metabolism. I swear, Newt, your stomach is like a black hole."

For the first time in several minutes, I looked up from our contraption, only to notice that Newt wasn't paying attention to me. He was looking at something over my shoulder.

Craning my neck to look in the same direction, I saw Gabe standing in the doorway watching us with an unreadable expression on his face.

Not that it was different from his usual expression. His face was almost always unreadable.

"Do you mind?" Newt said, his voice flatter than usual. "We're trying to get this finished before Sebastian wakes up."

His hands were occupied holding the last pieces of our contraption together, so Newt stretched out his leg and closed the bedroom door with his foot.

Gabe didn't say a word as it slammed in his face.

Newt didn't ask me about the argument, and I didn't feel inclined to talk about it either. We just passed each other an understanding smile and set to work finishing our project.

A few minutes later it was finally done. Sebastian's leg was secured safely in the new traction frame, and he hadn't even woken up when we made the transfer.

"Whew. Another crisis averted," Newt said as we admired our handiwork. "I don't know about you, but I'm beat."

"I know," I agreed. "I think an early bedtime is calling my name tonight."

"Same," Newt nodded. "Although, first, I think a shower is needed. And then I'm raiding the pantry now that we've got some proper food in this place. See you in the morning?"

I shrugged as I opened the bedroom door. "Of course. Where else would I be?"

Newt really was an angel. No matter what was going on, he had a magic ability to make everything seem like it was going to be okay.

Maybe that was why he ate so much. It took a lot of energy to stay positive all the time.

My good mood lasted until I reached my own bedroom.

"Oh, hell no."

I'd been so focused on getting Sebastian taken care of that I'd forgotten one crucial fact. Gabe and I were still sharing a bedroom. He sat on the edge of the bed, scrolling through something on his phone, but he immediately looked up when I opened the door.

Our eyes locked for one tense and silent moment. Then I threw my hands in the air.

"Nope."

After our earlier argument, there was no way I was sleeping next to the man that night. No pillow wall would ever be high enough for me to relax with him so close by.

I needed some space. At least for one night.

The keys to the RV still sat like a lead weight in my pocket. Making a quick decision, I grabbed what few articles of clothing I owned and headed for the door.

I had hoped that Gabe would let me go without another fight.

I was wrong.

"Where are you going?" he demanded as he followed me.

My teeth clenched so hard I was barely able to spit out one single word.

"Out."

I stormed right through the front door and out toward the RV. My hands shook and I fumbled with the keys, which made a loud jangling sound in the otherwise silent forest.

GABE

Just as I managed to unlock the door to the RV, the keys were snatched from my hand.

"You can't leave," Gabe said, waving the keys in front of me like an accusation.

I tried to snatch them back, but I wasn't fast enough. "I'm not leaving. I'm just sleeping out here tonight."

Gabe stuffed the keys into his own pocket, where I would have no chance of retrieving them unless I wanted to go rooting through his pants. "No. You're safer inside. You need to stay there."

At least I'd already managed to unlock the RV. Giving up the keys as a lost cause, I pulled open the door, but Gabe blocked my path before I could set foot inside the RV.

"Would you fucking back off," I shouted as I shoved ineffectively at his chest. I may as well have punched a marble statue for all the good it did. "I don't care if it's safer inside. I need some space."

Finally, I was able to read one of the man's expressions. Oddly enough, he seemed baffled. It was like he couldn't understand why his claim that it was safer inside hadn't immediately won the argument.

"Are you doing this on purpose?"

In the face of such a strange question I nearly forgot my anger.

"What are you talking about?"

"This." He gestured to me, the RV, and the house like it was supposed to mean something. "Disobeying. Putting yourself in danger. Are you doing it on purpose?"

I laughed in his face, and the sharp sound of my voice startled a few birds from their trees. "What do you expect? That we're supposed to just obey you when you're keeping us like prisoners here. No. Worse than that. Prisoners are at least allowed the luxury of shampoo. We're just dolls to you. Something that you can box up and put away on a shelf while you go off and play the big badass hero all on your own."

I shoved him again and this time actually managed to make the man stumble back a step. Taking my opening, I pushed past him into the RV.

"I don't know why you're surprised. Anyone would be mad after you belittled them like that. I've given up everything to help my friend. I didn't even get to say goodbye to my family before being dragged out here, and I haven't said one word of complaint about it. Yet you still accuse me of being irresponsible. Of being selfish. Fuck that."

I stood in the door to the RV, filling the space with my body in case Gabe tried to follow me inside.

"I'm sorry I'm not the obedient soldier you would prefer, but you're just going to have to deal with that. Now, leave me alone."

Then I slammed the RV door closed before he could try to continue arguing and locked it from the inside. The sudden burst of emotion had my heart racing and I sat on the floor of the RV, waiting to see what would happen.

A few moments of silence passed where my pulse slowly calmed down. Eventually, I heard the faint sound of footsteps leaving and I watched through the RV window as Gabe went back inside the house.

I collapsed on the floor as a whole new barrage of emotions hit me. Tears that I had been holding back for days finally broke free from the dam I'd trapped them behind and flooded my eyes.

It wasn't fair.

I'd sacrificed so much without complaining. I'd done everything that was asked of me, and even gone above expectation. Yet somehow, once again, I wasn't enough.

The minute I had my own thoughts, took my own actions, suddenly I became an ungrateful brat and none of my previous efforts mattered.

My parents and Gabe would probably get along like a house on fire.

That was a bad analogy, considering the apartment we were living in had literally been blown up and burned down.

Although, maybe that made it an even more accurate comparison.

The words I'd said to Gabe continued to echo in my head. I hadn't told my parents goodbye. I hadn't told anybody that I was leaving. The only person I would have told was Newt, and he was coming with us so there was no point.

If I never returned from this little adventure, would anyone notice?

My therapy patients had probably already been reassigned. I only talked to my parents once a month, and they may not care if I missed a month.

My landlord might not even notice,

since I had no idea what happened with the apartment I shared with Newt once we went into hiding. Gabe had vaguely mentioned that it would be taken care of, but I had no idea what that meant.

So, the answer to my question was obvious. No one would notice if I never came back. At least, not for a while.

Wiping the tears from my eyes, I shed my clothes where I stood. I climbed onto one of the RV beds and wrapped myself in blankets. The wind whispered against the walls, like a dozen grasping hands trying to find a way inside my little haven of warmth.

I buried my head deeper into the bedding to try and block out all the sounds around me.

When I couldn't hear anything but the rushing of my own blood in my ears, I was finally able to relax a bit. One of my hands carded through my braids and traced over the familiar line of a scar running along my scalp. It extended from a spot just an inch behind my ear all the way to the back of my head. I'd had the scar for years, and most days I forgot it even existed. Every now and then, however, something would remind me of it, and then it was all I could think about.

I tucked my hand under the pillow before I gave in to the urge and started scratching at the line of uneven scar tissue.

It was a reminder of the last time someone other than Newt had noticed my absence.

CHAPTER SEVEN

Frankie

MORNING CAME FASTER than I wanted. It was a restless night tossing and turning on the uncomfortable bed, and when the sun peeked through the trees, I didn't feel any more rested than the night before. I was tempted to stay in bed all day, until a knock on the RV door disrupted me.

"All right. All right." I assumed it was Newt coming to check on me and didn't bother to put on any more clothes than the boxers and undershirt I'd fallen asleep in.

This decision turned out to be a mistake when I opened the door and found Gabe standing there in the early morning sunlight.

I would have slammed the door right in his face, but he placed a hand on the door to block it before I could.

"Wait. Please."

He held out a plate in front of him.

I wasn't sure what I found more distracting. The word "please" coming out of his mouth, or the plate of eggs and bacon made exactly how I preferred.

My stomach growled. Still scowling, I snatched the plate from his hand.

"You have five minutes."

After I put on a pair of pants, we ended up sitting around the small bench table in the RV. It was an awkward position. The size of the table meant there was no way to sit without our knees knocking. I tried to ignore it and focused on my breakfast as I waited for Gabe to figure out what he wanted to say.

"I was an ass yesterday."

I looked up at him with surprise, and a piece of bacon hanging halfway out of my mouth.

That was not how I imagined the conversation would start. If anything, I had expected him to try and convince me that the whole argument was actually my fault.

Swallowing my mouthful of food and chasing it down with several heavy gulps of orange juice gave me enough time to get over my shock. When I was finally able to talk, my words came out clear.

"Yes, you were."

The fact that he was taking responsibility for his actions was a good start, but if he wanted forgiveness, he was going to have to give me a proper apology first.

Gabe sighed and nodded, like he'd already expected that response. "I shouldn't have said what I said, and I'm sorry. It was uncalled for, and wrong. You're not unfit to be a physical therapist. I was just worried, although that's no excuse."

He was saying all the right things, but the way he spoke made the apology sound rehearsed.

The eggs on my plate had been steamed instead of fried or scrambled, which is how I knew Newt had made the breakfast. It wasn't the most common way to prepare eggs, but I hated the crispy edges that they got when fried and I didn't like mixing the whites and the yolks together to make scrambled.

Newt must have encouraged Gabe to come talk to me. He'd probably even helped Gabe plan out what to say and told him that offering of food would be the best way to get me to listen. He wasn't wrong. I hadn't eaten much the day before—which may have contributed to how angry I got—and the food definitely helped me think more clearly.

Most importantly, I trusted Newt. He wouldn't have helped Gabe plan an apology if he thought the other man wasn't sincere.

I pointed my fork at Gabe. "You claim you were worried, but we've been in hiding for weeks and you've never been that rude before. What changed?"

He eyed my fork, which was pointed right at the center of his forehead. "You're right. Yesterday, I... found one of the moles in my agency and managed to get some information out of him."

I didn't want to know what that meant, and resolutely kept any questions about the identity of this mole or how Gabe *questioned* them to myself. Instead, I only asked about the information he'd learned.

GABE

Gabe placed a folder on the table, careful to keep it far enough away from my breakfast to avoid stains.

Flipping open the file, I was greeted with a picture of a man I didn't recognize. He was a large man, with a big barrel chest and sloping shoulders. It was the kind of largeness that came from strength, even if his muscles were hidden under a healthy layer of fat.

His hair may have once been red but was now so gray that the original color was indistinguishable.

"Is this supposed to mean something to me?"

"Probably not," Gabe said, though he tapped the paper to draw my attention to the man in the photo anyway. "His name is Robert McLeod, and based on the information I've procured, he's the man running the pedophile ring that's trying to kill us."

That info did make the image of the man look a little more threatening, but the picture still meant nothing to me.

"I thought the Mafia King that Sebastian and Damien have history with was the one running the pedophile ring."

"The Mariano family is definitely

bankrolling the pedophile ring in some way, but they're not in charge of it. Damien is off finding a way to get rid of David Russo once and for all, but I'm afraid that wouldn't stop this pedophile ring. They would still exist, and they would still be trying to kill all of us. If we want to be safe, we need to get rid of this person as well. One way or another."

In my mind, the people trying to kill my friends—and by extension, me—were a group of amorphous and shadowy villains. Like the kind of boogeyman monster children were warned about in old fables. To see that the person hunting us was just a man like any other, was simultaneously both a letdown and also very disturbing.

Humans shouldn't be capable of such monstrous actions.

"I still don't understand. Why are you so worried? Shouldn't knowing who this person is be a good thing? Now you know who to go after."

Gabe sighed and pushed his glasses higher up his nose. He didn't always wear them. They seemed to be mostly for reading paperwork.

I wished he would wear them more

often. They gave his face more character and turned him from an emotionless rock to a stern school teacher with a secret badass side.

Of course, I would never say such a thing to his face. Then he'd probably never wear the glasses again.

"It's because I know who this man is that I'm worried. I'm not sure that he can be brought down."

"A bad guy with bad connections?"

Pinching the bridge of his nose, Gabe shook his head. I noticed for the first time that there were dark bags hanging under his eyes. The man looked like he'd gotten the same amount of sleep I had.

None.

"Robert McLeod definitely has mob connections, though nothing has ever been proven. But that's not what I'm worried about. It's his legitimate connections that concern me. He's got a lot of relatives in influential positions of government. He recently earned the title of Senator and there's talk of him running for president in a few years. Quite frankly, I'm not sure it's even possible to take this man out. Not without pissing off a huge portion of our government. Even if we could, it would take an army. I'm just one man, and at the moment I don't have any backup."

Tucking the picture back inside its folder, Gabe collected the whole thing and carefully set it aside. "So, I've decided, there's only one choice. You need to learn to defend yourself."

I choked on my last bite of egg. "Excuse me."

"There's no way I'm getting anywhere near Robert McLeod on my own. I'm going to need help, and that means I'll be leaving this safe house more often than planned. I need to know that you'll be able to defend yourself when I'm gone."

"Okaaaay..." The singular word stretched between my teeth, like it was trying to escape but I wasn't quite ready to let it go. "What exactly would that entail? Because I'll tell you right now, I'm not handling any guns."

"No guns," Gabe assured me. "I wouldn't have time to train you enough for you to use them with any efficiency. Nor do we have a safe shooting range for practice. No. We'll just stick to basic defense. Are you done?" He pointed down at my empty plate.

As much as I wanted to argue, or come up with another excuse to think for a moment, I had nothing left. So, I merely nodded.

"Good. Come on."

Leaving the plate still sitting on the table, Gabe dragged me out of the RV and into the clearing surrounding the safe house.

"Wait a minute," I said when he took off his jacket and hung it over a tree branch. "You mean we're doing this right now?"

"Yes. The sooner we get started, the better."

He unbuttoned his cuffs and rolled up his sleeves to reveal his forearms. It was easy to forget since he was always so buttoned up, but under his stiff exterior and formal suits, the man was well built.

Based on the rigid lines of muscle running down his forearms, he definitely hadn't skimped on his workouts since leaving the army.

Watching him get ready for whatever "lesson" he had planned made me feel like I needed to be doing something. I stood there in just a pair of slightly too big sweatpants and an undershirt, so I didn't have anything to remove. So, I did the only thing I could and tied my braids back into a ponytail. The familiar action always helped me get into the right mindset for work. Maybe it would help here as well.

"Okay, so what? You want to teach me how to fight?" I raised my fists into what I thought was a fighting stance. "All right. I guess we can give this a go."

Gabe immediately pushed my hands back to my sides. "That's not what we're doing. There isn't enough time for you to get proficient in hand-to-hand combat. Plus, you shouldn't be fighting anyway. No, what I'm going to teach you is how to escape."

"Escape?"

The day had only started, and it kept getting weirder.

"Yes, escape," Gabe agreed as he removed his glasses and stored them in a pocket of his jacket. "Right now, your job is not to fight. Your job is to survive. If someone comes after you, you get away and you run." His gaze briefly traveled up and down my body. "You've got long legs for your height. You should be good at running."

I nervously scratched at the back of my head, and my fingers automatically found the raised edge of the scar hidden under my braids. "I used to run track in high school."

The admission was barely loud enough to be heard over the sound of the rustling leaves. I wasn't even sure Gabe heard me, for he gave no reaction. Instead, he studied me for a moment before suddenly grabbing my wrist in firm grip.

"If someone grabs you, what do you do?"

"Um..." I hesitated.

Was this a test?

Was this something I was already supposed to know?

When I didn't respond, Gabe yanked on my wrist so I stumbled toward him.

Not knowing what else to do, I tried to pull back. It was useless. His hand easily wrapped around my entire wrist and clamped down with a grip as strong as iron.

However, this seemed to be the response that Gabe expected, because his lips twitched up into a slight smile.

"Exactly. When people are grabbed like this, their first instinct is always to pull back and try to put space between them and their attacker. However, this just pushes your wrist more firmly into my palm. Instead, you want to twist your wrist and pull against the weakest part of your attacker's grip, where the thumb and fingers meet."

He walked me through the motion several times, showing me how to twist and pull in one fluid motion. It took some fumbling, but eventually, I was able to remove my wrist from his grip even with him holding on tight.

"Huh. How about that." I examined my wrist. It was a little chaffed from the friction between our skin, but I was free with minimal effort. "Wasn't expecting that to work."

Gabe grabbed my other wrist. "It just takes practice, but the principle is the same no matter how someone grabs you."

We spent a half hour going over different ways to escape a wrist grab. Right wrist. Left wrist. Straight on. From the side.

By the end of it my wrists were chafed raw, but I felt more comfortable with the technique.

After that, we moved on to other ways

a person might try to grab me. The upper arm. The shoulder. Even the lapel. In all of them, the principle was the same, just executed in slightly different ways.

Compromise my attacker's grip and use the opening to get away.

I was almost feeling confident in my ability to escape until, without warning, Gabe grabbed me in a full bear hug from behind and literally lifted me off the ground.

"This isn't as common, but if your attacker is much larger than you or trying to kidnap you, they might try to pick you up like this."

His breath was right in my ear. I could feel the vibration of every word, and I instinctively shivered. Goosebumps ran over my skin, and this time it wasn't from the cold air.

"What am I supposed to do here? I can't twist my whole body around. I can barely move my arms."

I squirmed to show how trapped I was, and immediately realized my mistake. The entire front of his body pressed right up against my back and the material of his shirt did little to hide the firm lines of his muscles.

Something hot clenched in my stomach, and I realized with growing horror that I was aroused.

"You can still move your arms a little," Gabe said, completely oblivious to my predicament. "From there, you should at least be able to reach my hands. Try grinding your knuckles over the tendons on the back of my hand."

I did, pressing as hard as I could, and I felt him flinch. His grip loosened enough for me to slide down to the ground and get my feet under me again, though he didn't fully let go.

"Good. The unexpected pain from such a move might make them let go entirely, but at the very least it'll loosen their grip. From there, just grab any of my fingers and bend them backward. I'll have to either let go, or let you break my finger. Either way, my grip is compromised, and then you can escape."

I didn't pull hard enough to hurt him, but I went through the motions to show I understood what he was talking about, and he let me go.

My palms were sweaty, and my breathing came harder than it should. I wiped my hands against my shirt, trying to ignore the heat rushing through my system and the tingling in my gut that wanted to blossom into something more.

It was fine. I just hadn't experienced much physical contact with anyone other than Newt and my patients for a while. Feeling aroused when someone was pressed up close to me was completely normal. It didn't mean anything.

I was so busy trying to calm myself down that I didn't notice Gabe inspecting me with a critical eye.

"You have long hair," he said, as if coming to a conclusion.

Before I could ask what he meant, his hand fisted in my braids and yanked my head back.

"The hair grab is a pretty common controlling move, especially against people with long hair, but getting out of it requires a different kind of technique. Instead of pulling away, you need to get closer."

He explained the process for getting out of a hair grab, but I didn't hear a word of it.

His hand pressed right against the scar on the back of my head. My brain short circuited and I couldn't move. Newt was the only one to ever touch that sensitive spot since I was a teenager, and the feeling of someone else's touch there sent a momentary wave of fear racing through me. Yet, at the same time, arousal still burned my veins, hotter than ever. I'd never considered myself to be someone who had a kink for hair pulling, but the prickling of my scalp as Gabe tugged at my braids was making my insides squirm in a way I'd never experienced before.

I remained frozen with indecision, torn between two conflicting reactions. Several moments passed where I didn't respond, and I could practically feel Gabe's confusion grow.

"Frankie..." He tugged my braids again, as if to remind me what we were doing. "Are you paying attention?"

"Uh..." My limbs suddenly started moving again, like someone had flipped a switch in my brain. I flailed, batting Gabe's hands away from me and putting space between us. "I think that's enough for today."

Luckily, he let me go. I had completely missed his explanation for how to get out of the hair grab. If he'd expected me to free myself, I would have been trapped.

"Enough?" Gabe looked toward the sky. "It's only been about an hour."

The fact that he could tell that just from the movement of the sun, even with so many trees blocking the way, was an impressive feat, but I wasn't in the right headspace to admire it. So many conflicting emotions still coursed through me, and I felt like I was about two seconds from fainting and getting an erection at the same time.

I needed to leave.

"Yeah, I, um..." I looked toward the house, where I thought I saw movement in the window. "I should check on Newt and Sebastian. See if they need anything. That is my job, after all. Right? As a physical therapist. Yeah, I'm just gonna..."

I pointed vaguely toward the house before making a quick retreat and bolting for the door of the house.

Newt was in the kitchen cleaning up the remnants of breakfast. My assumption that he had been the one to send Gabe out to me with food and an apology had been right, but I couldn't even gloat about it.

"Everything okay?" Newt asked as I walked past.

"Fine," I said without looking at him. "Just... bathroom."

I kept walking and shut myself in the bathroom, one of the few places in the small house where I could get a moment of privacy.

Gabe's papers and laptop took up almost every flat surface, including the floor. I stepped carefully over them and sat on the edge of the tub.

Rubbing my hands over my face, I tried to calm down.

What had happened back there?

I'd never reacted like that to someone. Granted, I didn't have many opportunities to get so physically close to people except for Newt and my patients, but I'd been on dates before. I'd even slept with a few guys, but none of them had created such an intense and confusing reaction in me.

In an ideal situation, I would distance myself from Gabe until I could figure out what it all meant. Unfortunately, our situation was anything but ideal.

I groaned when I remembered the sleeping arrangements. Unless I wanted to sleep in the RV again—which Gabe was right about, it wasn't safe for me to be so far away from the others—then I would be sleeping next to him at night.

That was going to make things a lot more complicated.

CHAPTER EIGHT

Gabe

TIME AT THE safe house never seemed to move properly. Everything seemed to be too fast and too slow all at once. My meeting with the director arrived as scheduled, and while I was eager to get it over with, I also wanted to delay it as long as possible.

I'd dealt with one mole in the FBI, but there were certainly others. So, I didn't trust letting anyone, not even the director, know which house we were staying at. That meant that in order to meet with the director, I would have to leave the safe house again.

Just the thought of leaving the others alone, of what could happen to them when they were unguarded, gave me anxiety. It was a new experience. I rarely felt anxious. Even back in my army days, I'd been known for my unshakable nerves. Yet now, I was fighting off the urge to pace just from the thought of leaving the people in the safe house unguarded.

Teaching Frankie some self-defense moves had helped calm my anxiety a little. At least he had a chance of getting away if someone tried to attack him. I'd wanted to keep up the lessons as much as possible while I had the chance, but after the first one, he didn't seem keen on continuing. Every time I brought it up, he found an excuse to do something else.

Some of the excuses had been pretty flimsy since there wasn't much to do in the house. He was obviously avoiding me, but I hadn't yet figured out why.

Was he still mad about our fight?

I'd apologized and he'd seemed to forgive me. Even Newt had assured me that Frankie wasn't still mad, and the little nurse didn't seem like the type to lie.

Something else must be going on. I'd never been very good at navigating social situations. It was why I always kept everything formal. Formal interactions had a set of rules I could follow. Casual interactions were messy.

Yet, living in such close proximity with three other people for so long, it was impossible to not make a mess eventually.

These thoughts plagued me all the way to my meeting with the director. Even as I pulled my car into a parking spot near the lake where we'd agreed to meet, my mind was still hyper-analyzing every interaction I'd had with Frankie over the last few days.

The director's greeting brought me out of my thoughts.

"Gabe. Glad you could make it. Sit down."

Director Thornton sat on a park bench overlooking a small lake. A wisteria tree draped its branches over the water on his right, and on his left a spot on the bench remained open and waiting for me.

"Are you actually glad, or are you just saying that?" I asked as I took the seat.

"I am glad," he said, though his eyes remained pointed forward toward the lake. "Though I wish the situation was different. This should be a formal meeting. Not something Lily has to arrange off the books."

"I would have preferred that too."

We sat in silence for a moment. The wind waved the wisteria branches like a curtain and several ducks floated by on the lake's surface.

"Why did you do it?"

The director's voice was flat. He could have been asking about anything.

Just for reassurance, I slipped a finger inside my own sleeve to feel the handle of the knife hidden there.

"Do what?"

The director huffed out a little laugh and shook his head. "The fact that I have to specify is a sign of how bad the situation has gotten. Let's start with your first offense. You kidnapped several people we were trying to place under witness protection."

I scanned the lake. There were a few people walking the path around the water and I automatically categorized them based on their potential danger level.

Not far away, a jogger dressed in colorful running gear was coming closer.

Danger level low. Even if they were an enemy trying to hide in plain sight, they would pick an outfit that allowed them to conceal more weapons.

"I didn't kidnap anyone. The Roth brothers, along with the two civilians, came with me willingly. Besides, you know why witness protection was a bad idea for them. It already failed the Roth brothers once."

A little farther down the path, a mother pushed a large baby stroller.

Danger level high. That stroller could be used to hide a variety of things, from a camera to an assault rifle.

Finally, Director Thornton turned to look at me. The situation was obviously causing him stress. He looked like he'd aged several years since I'd seen him last.

"At first, I was suspicious of the Roth brothers. They were only a little more than teenagers when they ran from witness protection the first time. Barely adults. Yet, they supposedly managed to stay off our radar and avoid the Mariano family. It doesn't seem possible for two people so young."

I looked away from my surveillance of the lake. "Supposedly?"

"I've had my suspicions..." he trailed off but didn't look away from me.

I gave him a moment to collect his words and returned to my surveillance.

On the opposite side of the lake, a man fed the ducks along with a young girl.

Danger level high. I wished I could say that a father feeding the ducks with his daughter wasn't suspicious, but with our current enemies being who they are, the presence of a child did not allay suspicion. There was no guarantee the girl was even related to the man, and they were positioned perfectly to have a clear view of both me and the director.

Eventually, Director Thornton found his voice again. "How could the Roth brothers have stayed alive for so long without help?"

My vision tunneled, and for a moment I saw nothing but the director's face. "You think the Roth brothers sold out to the Mariano family and are now working for the man who killed their parents?"

"It would make sense," the director shrugged. "Grudges fade over time, and constantly living on the run gets tiring. If David Russo extended them amnesty in exchange for their services, the offer might look tempting."

I'd never heard anything so idiotic.

Both Damien and Sebastian Roth hated David Russo with a passion and would never work for him. However, before I could argue that, Director Thornton interrupted me.

"But as I said, that *was* my suspicion. I have a new one now." He looked at me again, and the stress melted off him. For a moment he looked like the commanding leader I'd always known. "Gabe. Why did you kill Agent Adder?"

Everything went silent. I couldn't even hear my own heartbeat. My blood felt like ice in my veins and my mouth opened and closed several times before it would work properly.

"I didn't kill him."

"Gabe," the director sighed. "He's dead. I saw the body myself. I know your handiwork. No one else patches up their victims while questioning them. What happened? Did you accidentally go too far? Or did you get everything you needed out of him, so you disposed of him?"

Every word out of the director's mouth made me angrier until I had no choice but to move, or else I would explode. I jumped off the bench and spun around to face the director. That put my back toward the open lake, leaving me vulnerable, but I didn't care.

"Blake was alive when I left him. Yes, I roughed him up. He was working for the Mariano family, and I needed answers. What was his cause of death? None of the injuries I caused would have killed him."

When I jumped up from the seat, the director pulled out his gun, which now pointed directly at my chest.

"That's what you're going with, Gabe? Blake Adder was the mole?"

I watched the gun. His finger was off the trigger, so he wasn't ready to shoot me yet. "Well, one of the moles. I'm sure there are others."

Instinct raised the hair on the back of my neck. The director's gun wasn't the only weapon pointed my way.

So many pieces fell into place all at once, it was like a picture suddenly bloomed in my mind.

"You think I'm the mole."

"Can you blame us?" the director said. His weapon never wavered. "Think about how it looks. You were living with the Roth brothers and had plenty of opportunity to plant that bomb in their apartment. Then you steal the witnesses away from witness protection and won't tell anyone where they are. After that, you immediately turn around and kill the agent who was investigating the attempts on the Roth brothers' lives. One of those things would be incriminating enough, but all together... I'm sorry, Gabe, but there's no getting out of this one."

My jaw ached from how hard my teeth ground together. "You really think I would work for David Russo? After the Mariano family killed my own sister?"

I nearly reached for my own weapon but managed to control my anger enough to keep my hands in plain sight. One wrong move from me would spell my end. There was no telling how many people had weapons pointed at me in that moment, or how twitchy their trigger fingers were.

The director's gun lowered a fraction, so it was no longer pointed directly at my heart. "There's no evidence that the Mariano family killed your sister. You're the only one who has ever made such a claim. For all we know, that could be a clever story for you to hide behind. Please, Gabe, just come quietly. There's no reason to make this worse than it already is."

What could I say to such an accusation?

There were no words to express the sense of loathing and betrayal that coursed through me.

"I'm not—"

That was as far as I got. Before I could utter more than two words, something wet and warm splattered my face. My vision was tinted red, but I could still see Director Thornton sitting on the bench just as he had been for our whole conversation.

Except now there was a hole blown right through his head.

The gun fell from his hand, and he slumped over on the ground.

I moved before I realized what I was doing and jumped behind the bench. Luckily, it was made of metal, or else I would have died as several more bullets lodged in the bench. Based on their size, they came from large caliber guns that would have pierced right through a wooden bench and taken my head with them.

There was no way to even know who was shooting. Bullets seemed to come from everywhere. No direction was safe.

The car. If I could just get to my car, then I could drive to safety.

I'd barely taken a step away from the bench and toward the parking lot when a bullet struck the ground right in front of my foot.

Not that way. I'd never reach the car before I was shot to pieces.

The wisteria tree might provide some cover. At least better than the meager bench.

Another bullet struck the ground only a few inches away. Too close for comfort. Taking a diving roll, I threw myself behind the nearby tree.

Every exit was cut off. I didn't even have to look to know. It was the first thing I would secure if I was running such a mission. To make sure my target had nowhere they could retreat. There would certainly be people guarding every path out of the park and even if I could get to my car, there would probably be people blocking the nearby streets.

In situations like this, my mind always wandered back to my days in the Army Rangers. We traveled through some tough terrain back then, and often had to get creative with the resources available to us.

I scanned my surroundings.

The lake took up most of the space. It provided open sightlines for those guarding the area, but also created a barrier that was impossible to traverse without a boat.

Almost impossible.

My gaze landed on a patch of hollow reeds growing out of the water near the edge of the lake and a plan began to form in my mind. It would be difficult, but it might be my only chance.

A bullet struck the tree near my face. I still couldn't see who was shooting at me, but they must be getting closer since the angle of their bullets was changing.

I had looked at a map of the area before coming here. The lake was relatively small but connected to a river. Maybe I could swim my way to safety. Water would stop the bullets from reaching me. I could use one of the reeds like a snorkel to stay safe below the surface.

It was a terrible plan.

A messy plan.

I hated mess, but I hated the thought

of dying even more.

What would happen to Frankie and the others if I never returned?

No, that wasn't an option. I had to survive. There was no time left to come up with a better plan. I would have to make this one work.

After counting to three, I bolted for the lake.

My sudden movement must have startled my attackers. The bullets stopped for a moment, but then started up again even more frantically than before.

Fire ripped through my shoulder. One of the bullets had found its mark, but I didn't stop running. Stopping would mean death.

I couldn't die here. Not when there were people waiting for me.

At the edge of the lake, I grabbed the sturdiest reed I could see and snapped it off at the root.

Then I dove into the water.

CHAPTER NINE

Frankie

"FRANKIE, SIT DOWN. You're making me tired just watching you."

Newt sat in a chair next to Sebastian's bed, changing the bandages wrapped around the other man's torso and arms.

Sebastian's lacerations and burns were healing nicely, the skin around the edges a healthy pink of new growth. While it was impossible to tell without an x-ray, his leg also seemed to be doing well. The pain had lessened and there hadn't been any more incidents after he fell out of bed the other day. Seeing Newt so worried must have humbled him, for he'd been a model patient ever since.

I wished I could be happy about his progress, but I was too stressed to feel anything but panic.

It had been two days since Gabe left to meet with the FBI director, and we hadn't heard a word from him since.

"How can I sit down? I feel like I'm going to explode." To emphasize the point, I swung my fists wildly as I paced back and forth across the small room. "A simple meeting shouldn't have taken this long. What if they arrested him? Or worse, what if he's..."

I couldn't bear to finish that sentence, but it echoed in my brain anyway.

What if he's dead?

No, it wasn't possible. Gabe was too strong, too smart, too damn stubborn to just die. Something else must have delayed him. Maybe he'd discovered a new lead on finding the people who were hunting us. Or maybe Damien needed help with something.

Yes, those were perfectly logical reasons why Gabe hadn't returned yet, so long as I ignored the silence of the phone clutched in my hand.

Gabe had left behind a second secure

cellphone to maintain communication while he was gone. It had taken him a few days to set up after we arrived at the safe house, but it worked now, so there was no reason for him not to call if something had changed.

Unless he couldn't call.

My thoughts came full circle, and I was back to fretting again.

With a sigh, Newt finished tying off the last of Sebastian's bandages.

Sebastian placed a hand over Newt's, thanking him with a smile, before his face fell back into a solemn expression.

"I should have gone with him."

Newt and I both immediately tried to argue, there was no way Sebastian was going anywhere in his condition, but the man just cut us off with a raised hand.

"I know I couldn't go with him like this. I've only just started sitting up on my own. I'd be no use to anyone."

He closed his eyes for a moment, holding back a deep well of pain and regret that made Newt squeeze his hand tighter.

"What I mean is that I shouldn't be injured like this in the first place. If I'd done things differently... been more careful with my investigation of the missing kids, or noticed an intruder in our apartment before they planted a bomb, then I could be helping Gabe now. He'd have some backup instead of having to handle everything alone."

I stared down at the phone in my hand, willing the screen to light up with an incoming call, but it stayed dark and silent.

"No, I should have gone with him."

On instinct, Newt reached out to grab my hand, but he didn't let go of Sebastian. A smile threatened to take over my face at the sight of Newt accidentally turning himself into an overstretched bridge of support.

"Don't be silly, Frankie. What could you do? You're not law enforcement or a detective. You don't have any combat training. There's nothing you could do for a meeting with the FBI director, especially if that meeting went wrong somehow."

With the phone in one hand and Newt holding the other, I couldn't do anything except growl in frustration under my breath.

"I'd at least be more help than I am here. Sebastian needs a nurse more than he needs a physical therapist right now. If I'd gone with Gabe, maybe I could have done something to help him."

"Or you could have hindered him even more." Sebastian spoke softly, with an apologetic look on his face, but he also didn't try to take his words back. "I'm sorry to be blunt, but unless you know what you're doing in a situation, it's best to stay out of the way."

He looked down at the bandages covering his body, and his leg wrapped in a cast from toe to hip.

"Even when you know what you're doing, sometimes things still go wrong. There's enough danger for all of us right now. We don't need to make things even harder."

Shaking off Newt's grip, I ran a hand through my braids and flinched when I felt one of them start to unravel.

"I'm not useless. I can help."

"I know, but—"

Before Sebastian could finish, I cut him off. "No. Don't placate me. I'm not a child. I just..." My fists clenched so hard I felt the edges of the phone press into my palm. "I need to go sit down."

It was the exact thing Newt had been

trying to convince me to do a few minutes ago, yet no one commented on my hypocrisy as I used it as an excuse to leave the room.

I first sought the solace of my bedroom, but it was a space I shared with Gabe. His side of the bed, somehow neatly made despite only having access to half the sheets, was a stark reminder of his absence. Instead, I tried to lock myself in the extra bathroom, but this was where Gabe had set up a makeshift office. I also didn't want to monopolize the main bathroom in case Newt or Sebastian needed it, and the kitchen was too open for privacy.

So, I turned to my tried-and-true hiding spot.

The RV.

When this whole adventure was over, I was going to miss the clunky vehicle. It had given me so much support during the second most trying time of my life.

Taking a deep breath, I curled up on the RV's bed. The phone remained clutched in my hand, still silent.

I stared at the dark screen.

"You stupid man. Where are you?"

Holding the phone to my chest, I lay

my head on the pillow, just intending to rest my eyes. I had barely slept in the last few days. Although my nerves were still strained with worry, my exhaustion won out in the end, and I fell asleep.

CHAPTER TEN

Frankie

THE SUN WAS still up when a knock on the RV door woke me, though the angle of the light was different. Either I'd slept an entire day, or it had only been a few hours.

Based on how groggy I felt and the grit clinging to my eyes, either option was a possibility.

"Frankie," Newt's familiar voice called through the door. "You awake?"

"Yeah, I'm up." My throat felt like it had been replaced with a tube of sandpaper and my eyes were sensitive around the edges. If I didn't know better, I would have thought I spent my entire time in the RV crying, but not a single tear had escaped me.

When Newt stepped through the door carrying a large glass of water, I groaned in relief. As soon as the drink was in my hand, cold condensation dripping over my fingers, I chugged half the glass in one go. I would have drunk more if it weren't for my need to breathe.

"Thanks," I gasped when I came up for air. "How'd you know I needed that?"

Newt shrugged. "I noticed you didn't eat or drink much these last few days. There's food prepared back in the house. Also..." He held up a bag with some supplies. A closer inspection revealed they were the hair care items I'd bought at the store the other day.

I sheepishly tugged at the braid that had mostly come undone. "Is it that noticeable?"

"Not really." Newt took my hand and led me out of the RV. "But you're more easily agitated when your hair needs to be redone."

Back inside the house, we went through the familiar motions of my hair care routine. Just taking out all the braids and washing and conditioning everything took over an hour, but it was much easier with two people than if I'd done it alone. Newt had been helping me with my hair for years, ever since our first semester of college when we became roommates. He'd noticed me struggling with my hair on my own and offered to help.

At first, I thought it would be simple. So long as I walked him through the steps, then everything would be fine.

How wrong I'd been.

The first time he tried to help with my hair, he messed it up so badly I had to go to a salon to get it fixed. My anger had quickly died in the face of his numerous apologies, and I eventually agreed to let him try again. With a lot of practice on his part, and patience on mine, he'd eventually gotten better.

Now, years later, Newt easily managed my tight curls without a second thought.

"Do you want the same braid pattern as before, or something new?"

I thought about it for a moment, while at the same time finishing the last few bites of food on my plate at the kitchen table. A new pattern did sound enticing, but there was already enough upheaval in my life right now.

"Keep it the same. We don't have the usual materials, so it's probably not the best time to experiment."

Newt started partitioning out the sections for the braids, using a chopstick we'd found in a kitchen drawer since we didn't have a proper stylist comb.

"So, do you want to talk about it?" he asked as his fingers deftly twisted the first braid into shape.

"Talk about what?"

I was glad he stood behind me so I couldn't see his disapproving look.

"About Gabe."

I shrugged, though I was careful not to move my head. "Not much to talk about. He's missing, and as you and Sebastian have so helpfully pointed out, there's nothing we can do about it."

The first braid was finished and hung against my neck. The feeling brought a sense of comfort. I always felt a bit naked when my hair was unbraided, like some sensitive part of me was exposed to the open air.

Newt ran some leave-in conditioner through the second lock of hair before he started braiding.

"Not about that. I'm talking about the fact that Gabe has obviously gotten under your skin. That's not like you. Normally you have an endless amount of patience, yet Gabe is constantly getting a reaction out of you."

I frowned. The downside to having Newt standing behind me meant I couldn't glare at him. "That's not true."

Newt stopped braiding for a moment to lean over my shoulder and look me directly in the eye, one eyebrow raised in an incredulous look. "Frankie. I once saw a patient call you a tar-baby and order you to go back to picking cotton, and all you did was laugh."

Ah, yes, Mr. Locklin. I remembered him. His family had warned me about him when they brought him to me for therapy. He was "raised in a different time" they'd said.

Even now, that phrase made me snort and roll my eyes.

Yeah, the man was raised in a time when the amount of melanin in a person's skin dictated the amount of respect they were owed.

Still, I'd eventually managed to win the

man over by not taking any of his crap. In the end, he'd listened to my instructions, and even seemed to have a higher opinion of me than his own sons.

"Getting angry at Mr. Locklin wouldn't have done anything except enforce his racist beliefs. Plus, I'm pretty sure half of his angry outbursts were fueled by dementia."

"True, but most people wouldn't have the patience to put up with that kind of mistreatment and find a way to work with him. You did."

The second braid was done and joined the first.

"So what? I'm good at my job. What's that got to do with anything?"

The chopstick dragged over my scalp as Newt sectioned off the next piece of hair. "Gabe's gotten more under your skin than any patient I've seen before. Why? He's hardly the most challenging person you've ever met. Half the things he does that make you mad aren't even that bad. So, I can't help but think there's something more going on."

Rather than demand an immediate answer, Newt let me sit in silence for a while as he continued to braid my hair. A quarter of my head was done by the time I finally responded.

"He reminds me of my family." Newt's silence, and the unceasing motion of his fingers in my hair, were all the encouragement I needed to continue. "They micromanaged everything I did. When I was younger, I thought it was their way of showing that they cared, since they weren't the most emotionally expressive people."

As Newt sectioned off the next lock of hair, he was careful not to let the point of the chopstick touch the scar on the back of my head.

The gesture was appreciated. Newt knew how much I hated having that spot touched, but the obvious avoidance only reminded me of its existence.

"However, when I actually needed them, it turned out that their protectiveness had nothing to do with love. It was just about control."

Newt finished off the braid and carefully moved on to the next lock of hair on the other side of the scar. "I think I get what you're saying, but it still doesn't answer my question. Surely you've encountered overprotective and controlling people before and you've never reacted so strongly. What makes Gabe different?"

When Newt finally finished braiding the area around my scar, I sighed in relief. "I think I'm afraid of being disappointed. Gabe could be better than my family was, but what if he's the same?"

Behind me I could feel Newt thinking, although his hands never stopped their work.

"I guess that's the risk of getting to know someone," he said after a moment. "They might let you down. But then again, they might not."

Grumbling under my breath, I refused to admit that Newt had a point. We finished my braids without any other issues, and I took a moment to admire them in the mirror. With my hair back in proper order, I felt more like myself again.

Newt placed a hand on my shoulder, while staying out of the mirror so he didn't block my view. "You should talk to Gabe. Like, really talk. Not that snarky thing you do when you're trying to keep someone at arm's length."

Running my hands through my braids

one last time, I let them fall loose around my neck, so they just barely touched my shoulders.

"We did talk for a bit when he brought me breakfast. You know, the morning you taught him how to apologize. That wasn't so bad."

I distinctly did not mention what else Gabe and I had done that morning. If Newt ever found out about my reaction to feeling the other man's body so close to mine, I'd never live it down. Just like I would never let Newt forget that he gave Sebastian an accidental lap dance when the two of them first met.

What are friends for, if not to tease each other relentlessly?

Before I could say anything else, I was cut off by the phone ringing. I'd never heard that particular cellphone go off before, and at first I didn't realize where the sound was coming from.

Why did it not surprise me that Gabe had chosen the most generic beeping sound as the ringtone?

Picking it up, I shoved the phone against my ear. "Gabe? You there?"

At first, I was met with only static and silence. Then, very faintly, I heard a single

word spoken in Gabe's familiar voice.
    "Frankie."

CHAPTER ELEVEN

Frankie

EVEN WHEN I pushed the accelerator all the way to the floor, the RV barely went above sixty. It took me several hours to drive out to the area Gabe had indicated, and I was a wreck the entire time. My hands felt numb on the steering wheel, and it took all my concentration to keep breathing evenly.

The sun had already been down for hours when I crossed over the border of a little one-stoplight town a hundred miles away from our safe house. Gabe's voice had sounded strange on the phone, slurred and difficult to understand. It had taken a lot of back and forth to come up with a basic idea of his location. Neither the RV nor the secure cellphone had GPS, so I'd had to figure it out using a paper map I'd found and Gabe's vague description.

In the end, all that effort turned out to be pointless. Gabe said he was at a bus stop, and the tiny town only had one.

A streetlight flickered with an uneven tattoo of sparking electrics, and barely illuminated the bus stop. The ramshackle structure looked like it was ready to fall down at any moment and was only identifiable as a bus stop by the small sign hanging from a single crooked nail.

I barely remembered to put the RV in park before I flew out of the door.

"Gabe."

A lone figure sat on the bus stop bench, slouching against the awning's support pillar like he was asleep.

Please, let him just be asleep.

The person had a coat draped over them like a blanket, so I couldn't immediately see their face, but they stirred at the sound of my voice.

I collapsed to my knees in front of the bench, crying with relief when the coat fell away to reveal familiar gray eyes.

"Oh my God, Gabe. You're alive." My hands fisted in his shirt and I started shaking him. "Don't scare me like that again. I thought that... I thought you were... Oh, you fucking ridiculous man."

I don't know what possessed me in that moment, but before I realized what I was doing, I pulled Gabe closer and kissed him. Pressure had been building in my chest like a bubble for days as I worried over him. Once I knew he was alive, the bubble popped, and all that tension had to go somewhere.

It was a particularly graceless kiss. Just a smashing of lips together with no art or skill involved at all. I tasted blood from where I'd cut my lip on my own teeth, but I didn't care. Nothing mattered in that moment except the feeling of Gabe's heart still beating under my hand.

As quickly as the moment of madness overcame me it left, and I realized what I was doing. I pulled back and stuttered out an apology.

"Oh, fuck, I'm sorry. What am I doing? That's not... I shouldn't... Sorry."

I expected outrage, or even confusion, but Gabe didn't say a word. Squinting to get a better look at him in the flickering light, I found gray eyes staring at me with an unfocused glassy appearance, like he wasn't really seeing me.

Then, right as I watched, Gabe's eyes slipped shut and he slumped forward so his head landed on my shoulder.

"Gabe? What?" I grabbed the man to steady him, and that was when I felt it. Gabe was burning up. Fever scorched his skin from the inside. It was a wonder I hadn't noticed it during the kiss, but I'd been too caught up in my own relief.

I shook the man, trying to wake him up. He mumbled something, but his head lolled on his shoulders like a broken puppet.

"Ah, shit. Let's... um, let's get you inside the RV. Come on, Gabe. Help me out. You're too heavy for me to carry that far.

Whatever infliction Gabe suffered, he remained just conscious enough to support some of his weight as I dragged him over to the RV parked beside the bus stop. Once inside, with the door locked, I laid Gabe on the bed at the back of the vehicle and started inspecting him.

His clothes were much more ragged

than when he left two days ago, torn in many places and covered with splotches of mud.

Because of that, I didn't immediately notice the blood staining his shirt around his right shoulder, which had dried to a similar brown color.

There was no way for me to remove the shirt from Gabe, so I just tore the fabric away. It was already so damaged, the fabric easily gave way under my hand, leaving Gabe naked from the waist up.

I had my answer.

I'd seen enough wounds during my career to recognize the bullet hole in his right shoulder. That alone wouldn't be a problem as the bullet had gone cleanly all the way through, however, the wound was clearly infected.

It looked like Gabe had tried to triage the wound himself using...

Was that dental floss?

Hardly a sanitary material, and if the wound hadn't been properly cleaned before he stitched it closed, then he'd just trapped the bacteria inside so it could fester.

For the infection to become so bad in just two days, it must have been severe.

Thankfully, I'd brought some first-aid supplies with me, just in case, so I could cleanse the wound, but it wouldn't be enough. Gabe needed antibiotics to get the infection out of his system and bring down the fever, and I didn't have any medicine that strong.

One thing at a time. I could worry about antibiotics afterward. First, Gabe's wound needed to be treated.

"Sorry, but this is going to hurt," I said to the unconscious man as I laid out my supplies.

He didn't respond, but I swore his brow furrowed for a moment, like he was thinking deeply.

The first step was to cut away the makeshift stitches. I didn't want to know what Gabe had used for a needle, but the stitches were surprisingly even despite being made from dental floss. Gabe's training as a medic in the Army Rangers had paid off.

I quickly snipped the stitches, and a pinkish-yellow mix of blood and puss oozed from the wound. The smell of infection was horrible, but I had trained myself to control my gag reflex years ago. Patients still in the process of healing would not feel comfortable with me if I made a disgusted face every time they came near.

Besides, while Gabe's wound was ugly, it wasn't the worst I had ever seen.

After using a generous amount of gauze and saline to cleanse the wound, I was finally able to get a good look at what I was dealing with. The bullet entry and exit wounds on either side of Gabe's shoulder were straight forward, leaving no ragged edges or excessive damage behind. The bullet had been large, but simple. Not as devastating as something like a hollow-point bullet, which expanded on impact to do as much damage to flesh as possible.

With any luck, Gabe should be able to heal from the wound with minimal consequences.

Assuming I could get the infection under control.

The flesh around the wound was bright red, swollen, and even hotter to the touch than the rest of him. Spidery lines extended outward from the wound, confirming my biggest fear.

The infection had leeched into his bloodstream. He was definitely going to need antibiotics.

I finished cleaning the wound, then packed it with fresh gauze, but didn't stitch it closed again. Stitches could come later, but for now the wound needed a chance to breathe and drain out the remaining infection.

With so much of my focus on his right shoulder, I didn't pay attention to his left side until I'd finished treating the wound and was making him more comfortable on the bed. A series of old scars ran down the length of his left arm, like tiger stripes. Based on their similar pattern, the scars must have all happened at the same time. Such a wound would have been devastating, maybe even career ending for someone in the military.

Once he was well, he could tell me all about it. I had a plan for how to help him. I just didn't like what I would have to do.

Half an hour later, the RV was stashed in an out of the way parking lot and I observed an empty pharmacy from the safety of a dark alley. The building was closed for the night, which was not surprising since it was nearly two in the morning.

"I can't believe I'm doing this," I mumbled to myself as I tied a relatively clean piece of Gabe's ruined shirt over my face.

Sticking to the shadows, and avoiding the spotlight of the nearby streetlamp, I slunk up to the pharmacy's back door and pulled out a set of lock picks. They weren't perfect tools. I'd made them in a hurry by pulling the springs out of one of the RV's chair cushions and bending the wire into the shape I needed. They would never be enough for a more complicated job, but the backdoor of the pharmacy was surprisingly simple.

This place must have been one of those small towns that didn't see a lot of crime for their security to be so lax.

I slipped the wire picks into the lock, and my fingers quickly remembered the familiar movements. Although I hadn't used the skill in years, it was even harder to forget than riding a bike, and barely a minute later the door clicked open.

An ominous beeping on the wall greeted me. The control panel for the alarm wanted a code, and I had sixty seconds to punch in the right numbers before it went off.

Not wasting a second of my countdown, I ran to the back of the pharmacy where the prescription medications were stored. The more dangerous medications, like narcotics, were kept under heavy locks. My paltry lockpicks would never have stood a chance. Luckily, the antibiotics I needed weren't nearly as valuable, and so weren't as protected. A simple padlock, similar to the kind used on high school lockers, was all that stood between me and my bounty. It took me longer to find the right cabinet than it did to get the thing open and grab several bottles.

I'd just shoved the last bottle into my pocket when the alarm went off. I slapped some cash on the counter—to at least ease my conscience about stealing—and ran out of the building.

I kept running until I was a few blocks away from the pharmacy, then ducked behind a dumpster in an alley to wait. My heart pounded in my ears, and I shook from head to toe, making the pill bottles rattle in my pocket.

I'd actually done it. While it wasn't the first time I'd broken into a place—a fact I tried not to think about too much—it was the first time I remembered feeling so nervous.

GABE

In the past when I broke into a place, I was usually desperate to feel anything at all. I'd never even stolen anything before. It had all just been for the thrill of doing something I wasn't supposed to.

A few minutes later, several police cars with blue and red flashing lights drove past. I stayed hidden, waiting for the commotion to die down. A basic breaking-and-entering, when the only thing stolen was a few bottles of antibiotics, wasn't a particularly noteworthy crime. The police wouldn't bother with it for long. All I needed to do was wait until the lights and sirens disappeared, and the night was dark and silent once again.

It was four am by the time I returned to the RV. My legs ached from kneeling in such a cramped position behind the dumpster for so long, but I was otherwise unharmed, and Gabe was exactly where I'd left him. He didn't seem to have twitched a muscle while I was gone. Even his hair was in exactly the same position.

"Hey, I'm back. I need you to wake up enough to take these pills. Then we can head back to the safe house."

I didn't know why I bothered to talk to him. The unconscious man couldn't hear me. Even when I managed to rouse him from his sleep, I wasn't sure how aware he was of anything happening around him. I managed to get him to swallow a couple of the antibiotic pills by literally putting them on his tongue and holding a glass of water to his lips.

He choked on the first few sips of water, which dribbled from the corner of his mouth, before he eventually swallowed the pills and almost immediately fell back asleep.

Breathing a sigh of relief, at least for now, I turned the ignition in the RV, the engine roaring to life, and started driving back to the safe house.

CHAPTER TWELVE

Gabe

EVERYTHING AROUND ME felt like it was moving when I woke up. I cracked my eyelids open, and I was looking at an unfamiliar ceiling.

No, wait, not unfamiliar. I'd seen it before.

But where?

Memories came back to me slowly.

Meeting with Director Thornton. His accusation, and then his death. The shoot out with unknown assailants. The feeling of a bullet tearing through my shoulder. Hiding submerged under the surface of the lake for hours as I swam to safety, breathing only through a thin reed.

But what happened after that?

I had a brief memory of making a phone call.

Sitting up on what turned out to be a bed, I groaned and clutched my shoulder. It hurt, but not as much as I expected, and the wound had been expertly stitched and bandaged.

Oh, now I recognized my surroundings. I was in the RV. Looking toward the driver's seat, I was unsurprised to find Frankie behind the wheel.

"You're awake," he said, sounding happy, though he never took his eyes off the road. "Hold on one moment."

I swayed with the change in momentum as Frankie pulled the RV to a stop at the side of the road. As soon as he turned the vehicle off, he joined me at the back of the RV and immediately started checking my wound. "Thank God your fever broke. How are you? We're about twenty miles from the safe house. Can you wait that long, or is there anything that needs to be taken care of now?"

Fever?

That explained why I felt so shaky.

GABE

When Frankie unwrapped the bandages, I got a good look at the damage. The first thing I noticed was the sign of infection. I remembered crawling from the lake with my whole arm and shoulder on fire and touching anywhere near the wound felt like I was being shot all over again.

"Is everyone all right?" I asked, directing my words to the top of Frankie's head as he was leaning down to inspect my shoulder. His braids looked better than before.

He froze and looked up at me, dark eyes wide enough to see the whites all the way around. Then he laughed, the sound coming mostly out of his nose like he wasn't sure if he should be controlling his reaction or not.

"Of course that's your first question."

My brow furrowed in confusion. I didn't know what time it was, or even what day it was, but one thing was clear. The people I was meant to be protecting had been left alone for much longer than expected. Of course I would want to know if they were all right.

Why was that surprising?

"Yeah," Frankie nodded as he returned

to his work. "We're all fine. Sebastian is even starting to show some improvement. You're the one we need to worry about right now. What happened? How much do you remember?"

I explained in detail about my meeting with the FBI director and the subsequent fallout. My memory was extremely clear about what had happened and didn't turn fuzzy until after I crawled out of the lake.

"Oh, yeah," Frankie laughed. "Spending hours submerged in a lake with an open wound will definitely do it. No wonder your wound got infected."

More memories were coming back to me. After escaping the park, I couldn't go back to my car as it was under surveillance, so I'd walked until I found a town. From there, I'd intended to catch a public bus to get back to the safe house, but it was late, and I missed the last bus for the night. The next one wouldn't come until morning. At first, I'd been prepared to wait, but the infection in my wound worsened rapidly until I didn't think I'd be able to stay conscious that long. So, I'd called Frankie and told him where I was.

It was honestly a miracle he'd managed to find me at all. By the time I called him, I was already struggling to stay conscious and wasn't very precise in my directions.

I checked the position of the sun through the RV's window. It was a few hours past sunrise. "I've been gone too long. We should return quickly in case something happens to the others. After this, there will be even more people looking for us."

Frankie finished applying the bandages but didn't immediately return to the driver's seat. "Wow. You are determined to prove me wrong, aren't you."

I didn't know what to say to that statement, so I just stared at him, silently willing him to explain so I wouldn't have to ask.

He sighed and shook his head like he was trying to get water out of his eyes. His braids swayed and knocked against each other before falling still.

"At first I thought you were just some emotionless soldier, following orders without any actual care for the people under your protection."

He looked at me, and for the first time I noticed how long his eyelashes were.

They framed his eyes nicely and highlighted his expressions.

"You aren't the first person to accuse me of being heartless."

If anything, it was a mild insult compared to some of the things I'd been called before. "Stone cold bastard" had been thrown my way more than once.

However, rather than agree with me, Frankie shook his head again and took a seat on the bed next to me. "The point is that I've realized I was wrong. You do care. So much so, that your very first question after waking up from getting shot is about the welfare of other people. In fact, I think you care very deeply, and this whole *automaton* persona you present to everyone is just a way to protect yourself."

He tipped his head on his shoulder, so he was smiling at me sideways.

"Tell me I'm wrong."

We were sitting close enough for our shoulders to brush, though he made sure to avoid my injury. My right shoulder still hurt terribly, but I couldn't help bringing my hand up to trace over the scars running down my left arm. It was a habit I'd picked up ever since first getting them years ago, and the action was now automatic whenever I found myself thinking deeply.

I also realized that I was shirtless, and that the scars were on full display. Frankie must have seen them but hadn't said a word about them.

"The way that you are... you make it easy."

I knew I'd said the wrong thing when Frankie leaned back to give me a strange look.

"Easy? Are you calling me a slut?"

I gaped at him, horrified by my own words. It was a common occurrence. Things that made sense in my mind often didn't sound how I thought they would once spoken out loud. It was why I usually chose to remain silent unless I was positive about the reaction my words would get. I'd hurt people in similar ways in the past, though this was one of the more egregious mistakes I'd made.

"No, I don't mean..." My fingers found the largest scar on my arm, which cut across my bicep just above the elbow. I traced the line over and over again as I grasped to find the right words. "You're bright. You offer hope. Like light at the end of a dark tunnel. Your personality makes it easy to care about you."

This time I got the words right, for Frankie's face lit up with a genuine smile rather than the sarcastic one he'd been using earlier.

"Aw. That's probably the nicest thing anyone's ever said about me. Now, let's get back to the safe house so you can see that everyone is fine."

He patted my leg, then stood from the bed so he could return to his place in the driver's seat. As the RV rumbled to life again, a new memory pushed its way through the fog of my fever.

A cool press of lips against my own fever hot ones.

Had I imagined it?

Possible. Hallucinations were a common fever symptom and made more sense than Frankie actually kissing me.

Still, I couldn't be sure. I brought my fingers up to my lips and could so easily imagine it was Frankie's mouth pressing against me rather than my own touch.

As I watched him steering the RV back onto the road, I fell back on my tried-and-true reaction. Since I didn't know what to say or how he would react, I chose to keep

GABE

my silence.

CHAPTER THIRTEEN

Gabe

EVERYONE WAS OKAY. In fact, they were more than okay. Newt and Sebastian were ecstatic when Frankie and I returned and were equally horrified when I recounted what had happened to me.

I waited a few days to ensure that our location at the safe house hadn't been compromised, but when no one came banging on our door trying to arrest us, or worse, I figured our hiding place was still safe for now.

Only then did I try contacting Lily. She may be the director's secretary—former director's secretary—but she was still one of the only people in the agency I trusted absolutely.

Our conversation had been brief. Apparently, there was chaos among the higher-ups as they scrambled to assign a replacement director. The only thing she was able to give me was a promise to eventually have more information about the situation, and a warning to lay low for a while. The director's death was, unsurprisingly, being blamed on me. My name had jumped to the top of the list of the FBI's most wanted people, and if I showed my face anywhere, an army of FBI agents would probably drop from the sky to arrest me.

Overall, things were not looking good.

I tried not to think about it as I focused on healing while I waited.

For the first time, I could truly sympathize with Sebastian's frustration. While I could still move around freely, my arm was kept in a sling to stabilize my shoulder while it healed, and even that small limitation was driving me up the wall.

"You're lucky," Frankie admonished me when he noticed my agitation over the sling. "The bullet managed to avoid hitting any bones. If it had, you'd be looking at a much longer recovery time."

I knew that. Bullet wounds had been one of the most common injuries I treated when I was in the Army Rangers. I knew everything there was to know about bullet wounds, but that didn't make it any easier whenever I instinctively tried to reach for something with my right arm and found it trapped against my side.

Several weeks passed in this way, caught between frustration and confusion.

Sebastian was able to move around the house with the help of a wheelchair, which had been a whole other adventure to procure, and had thrown himself back into the case of stopping the pedophile ring and finding the missing children.

With nothing better to do, I helped. We moved my makeshift office from the bathroom into the kitchen, resolutely ignoring the glares from Newt and Frankie who would prefer we spend our time resting. Neither of us could sit still any longer, however, and we went over every detail we knew looking for some new thread to follow.

"So, this man, Robert McLeod, is

supposedly the one running the pedophile ring," Sebastian reiterated for the thousandth time while pointing at a picture of the man. "A fucking Senator who is able to manipulate the very laws of this country, is the one behind everything. No wonder we were never able to get a strong foothold on this case. Our enemy has literally every advantage. Although, that does make me wonder. If he's got all this money and all this power, why is he relying on the Mariano family for funding?"

I spread the various files and photographs over the table like a collage of crime, trying to piece together a larger picture from all these pieces. "Because he's such a public figure. All that money and power comes at the cost of anonymity. People would notice if he was spending large sums of money on seemingly nothing. We're never going to get anywhere focusing on the leaders of this ring. They're too well protected. Our best bet will be to focus on the underlings."

I moved the picture of Tansie Bell's son to the center of the table. "This boy. We need to focus on this boy. He's an anomaly."

Sebastian picked up the picture, studying it as if he'd never seen it before despite being just as familiar with everything on the table as I was. "What's so odd about him? It fits everything we know about how this pedophile ring works. A disadvantaged mother gives her kid up for adoption, and certain hospital administrators are paid to erase paperwork and make the child disappear from the system. The only odd thing is that Miss Bell happened to run into the kid by accident. Assuming he actually is her son, which we don't know for certain, that still doesn't tell us anything."

"Maybe it does." On my laptop, I brought up a map of the area where Tansie Bell's son was seen. "Why was the boy brought out in public? I could understand if there was a hotel nearby and they were bringing the boy to a... client." Sebastian and I both made a disgusted face. "However, this area is mostly historical buildings where tourists gather to take pictures, along with a bunch of shops and restaurants. If this kid is a victim of a pedophile ring, to them he is basically chattel. He's a product for them to sell, and this doesn't seem like the kind of place worth risking their product by bringing the boy out into the open."

Sebastian turned my laptop around so he could get a better look at the screen. "You think there's something special about this area?"

"I definitely want to go and visit the area myself. Get a look with my own eyes. A map can only tell us so much."

"And that's where I'm going to have to cut you off," Frankie's voice interrupted us. He stood over the table, his shadow falling across the collage. "Neither of you are going anywhere."

Over his shoulder, I could see Newt standing just a few feet away, arms crossed and tapping his foot with a disgruntled expression on his face.

Sebastian must have noticed Newt as well, for he immediately turned placating. "We weren't planning on going anywhere *right now*," he said, waving his hands in front of himself like a shield. "We just mean that *eventually* we want to visit the area."

I re-stacked the pictures into a more orderly layout. "There's nothing stopping me from visiting it right now."

Frankie snatched the picture of Tansie Bell's son from my hand. "Nothing but that hole in your shoulder. You're not going anywhere until you're healed."

I tried to grab the picture back, but he danced out of my reach. "It's been weeks. I'm fine."

"You are better than you were," Frankie agreed. "But that is not the same as fine. Now, go wash up so we can have dinner. Take a break from all this."

He stormed away from the table, taking the picture with him.

I followed after him, hissing under my breath when the sudden movement jolted my arm. Maybe I wasn't as fine as I claimed, but I wasn't about to let anyone know that, and refused to let the pain show on my face.

"This is my job," I said as I followed Frankie into our shared bedroom. "I can't just take a break from it."

"Well, maybe you should. Your job almost got you killed, and your own coworkers are now the ones hunting you down. As if being targeted by a mob-funded pedophile ring isn't bad enough."

Not wanting to let the others hear us

arguing, again, I turned to close the bedroom door. As I did so, I caught a glimpse of Newt and Sebastian talking. Based on their body language, Newt was obviously just as upset as Frankie, but somehow the pair managed to discuss their problem without arguing.

How did they do it?

Does being romantically involved make things easier?

Or are they both just that much better at communicating?

Sucking in a deep breath, I closed the door and turned to face Frankie.

"I cannot just give up on my job. That would mean giving up on all the victims who need my help, and I refuse to do that. And unless I have seriously misjudged your character, I don't think you want that either."

The fight instantly drained out of him, and he seemed to sag within his own skin. "No. I don't. I just wish that helping people didn't have to come at the risk of your own safety." He stepped forward until his head rested on my uninjured shoulder. "Sorry. I didn't mean to get mad at you. I just... hate everything that is happening right now."

A man putting his head on my shoulder was a request for comfort, right?

I'd never had anyone act so familiarly with me before, not since I was a kid anyway, and I didn't immediately know what to do.

Raising my arm that wasn't trapped in a sling, I stroked a hand over the back of his head.

I immediately knew that was the wrong move. Frankie sprang away from me, clutching the back of his head like I'd struck him. Panic made his eyes glitter in a way that should not have looked so pretty, and I realized I'd seen this expression on his face before.

"Are you injured?"

"What?" Frankie ran both hands through his braids in a self-soothing gesture as he took a deep breath. "No. Everything's fine. What makes you say that?"

"You reacted the same way when I grabbed your hair, back when I was trying to show you some self-defense. Is it something that I'm doing wrong? If I'm hurting you, then I want to know so I don't do it again."

For a moment it looked like Frankie

might bolt out of the room, and I was already prepared to face a reality where he locked himself in the RV again. However, rather than run, he sighed deeply and closed his eyes, tipping his head up toward the ceiling like he was praying. Then, when he opened his eyes again, there was a new strength in his expression.

Without saying a word, he grabbed my hand and pressed it against the back of his head, guiding my fingers to bury in his braids until I touched his scalp.

A thick line of knotted scar tissue ran along the back of his head. At first, I wanted to pull back, afraid I would hurt such an obviously sensitive area, but Frankie grabbed my wrist with both hands.

"It's fine. I don't actually feel anything there. You can touch. It won't hurt me."

With his permission, I slowly traced my fingers over the scar. It took the entire length of my hand to cover it, stretching all the way from just behind Frankie's ear to the back of his head. The fact that the scar was so raised meant that the wound had not been easy to stitch together, and the skin had not aligned properly.

A scar like this anywhere on the body would be a big deal, but on the head, it was even more shocking. I could imagine several different wounds that would leave such a scar, and each possibility left me feeling angrier than the last.

It was a struggle, but I managed to keep my voice steady as I spoke. "What happened?"

The wound may be old but the memories of it were obviously still raw as phantom pain flickered in Frankie's eyes.

"Oh, you know. An openly gay black boy living in the American deep south. High school was a treat."

He obviously needed a minute to collect his thoughts, so I guided us both to sit side by side on the bed. Not once did he ask me to remove my hand from his head, and I didn't feel particularly inclined to let go, so I just kept rubbing along the line of the scar as if I could erase it from his skin.

"I told you that I used to be on the track team in high school, right?" Frankie asked when he found his voice again.

I understood social cues enough to understand that he was not looking for an actual answer. It was just a transition into the story he actually wanted to tell. So, I nodded in encouragement for him to keep talking, but stayed silent as I listened.

"I didn't really like running on the track team, but I was good at it, and a sports scholarship was the only way I was going to college. I don't think I ever saw my parents so happy as the day I was told that I'd gotten the scholarship they wanted."

"You were injured because you earned a sports scholarship?"

I shouldn't have spoken. My role in this interaction was to listen, not to interrupt, but the idea was so absurd I couldn't help seeking clarification.

Luckily, Frankie didn't seem to mind the interruption. He merely laughed a sad little chuckle and pressed his head closer into my hand like a dog asking to be petted.

"The scholarship probably didn't help, but it wasn't the main problem. No, the main problem was the high school's locker rooms."

I moved on from gently rubbing his scar to giving him a full head massage. It seemed to calm him down, and he even moaned a little as he continued his story.

"The other boys weren't happy about having to shower and change around me. Most of them just avoided me, but there was this one guy. I'm not going to name him, because he doesn't deserve that recognition, so let's just call him dick-waffle, because I've always liked that insult."

It was certainly a descriptive insult. I could already picture the kind of person Frankie was describing.

Frankie's eyes were closed, and he looked serene as he enjoyed the head massage. The image was such a contrast to what he was saying that it gave me vertigo as I listened to him.

"Dick-waffle would not leave me alone. All through high school he was constantly harassing me, especially in the locker rooms when I couldn't get away from him so easily. Calling me a slut. Accusing me of creeping on the other boys when they were changing. Constantly demanding to know how many guys I'd fucked. I once tried to explain that I was still a virgin at the time, but that was a mistake. It only encouraged him."

The more I heard, the more I hated

where this story was going. Considering it ended with Frankie getting injured, I already knew I wouldn't like it, but this was worse than I expected.

"That's sexual harassment. Why didn't any of the adults stop it?"

Frankie opened his eyes just enough to raise an incredulous brow at me. "You grew up privileged didn't you? The teachers and staff at the kind of school I went to did not get paid enough to care. And my parents... well, I wasn't being physically harmed, my grades were still good, and I earned the scholarship they wanted. As far as they were concerned, I just needed to endure it and not rock the boat."

For the first time, I was glad for the sling on my arm. It hid the shaking of my fist. The hand on Frankie's head stayed gentle, but the other hand clenched so tightly in anger that the tips of my fingers were going numb.

Yet, Frankie continued like there was nothing unusual about what he said. "I managed to do what they wanted until the end of my senior year. I was so close to being done. My bags were already packed for college, but I just couldn't take it anymore. He started up his usual harassment in the locker room and I turned it back on him. I got flirty, and pointed out that his obsession with my sex life obviously meant that he wanted to sleep with me."

He laughed again, but I didn't find anything funny.

"Looking back on it now, I probably hit the nail on the head. Internalized homophobia is a bitch. Well, later that day, dick-waffle caught me alone when I was heading home and…" Frankie turned his head, so it pressed against my good shoulder. "He was on the baseball team and he had one hell of a swing."

I couldn't help it. I removed my hand from Frankie's head to instead cup his face and force him to look at me. "He attacked you with a baseball bat just because you flirted with him?"

"Yep," Frankie smiled, even as unshed tears gathered in his eyes. "Cracked my head clean open and left me lying on the pavement."

His words were so upbeat they sounded manic.

"My parents kept me on a tight schedule, so they noticed right away when

I didn't come home. It was a good thing they found me so quickly or I would have died. One of the benefits of overprotective parents. My motor functions were really screwed up for a while, and because of that, I lost my scholarship. But I didn't actually like track, anyway, so it was fine. My parents basically gave up on me, but in exchange, I got a really awesome physical therapist. She was a saint and helped me through a really hard time. I even became a physical therapist because of her, so you could say that dick-waffle actually did me a favor."

He was rambling and laughing at the same time as tears dripped from his eyes. I didn't know how to make him stop crying or calm him down, so I did the only thing I could think of.

I kissed him.

It was only meant to be a brief exchange, just enough to stop him from spiraling, but once we started, I couldn't seem to stop.

Just a moment ago I had been thankful for the sling, but now I hated it. With only one functioning arm, I could pull him closer, but I couldn't cradle the back of his head at the same time, as I so desperately wanted.

After a few moments locked together, Frankie seemed to come to his senses and pulled away. He didn't leave the embrace of my arm, but he put distance between his mouth and mine.

"What are you doing?"

I couldn't stop staring at his lips, wet with my saliva, but I forced myself to look him in the eye. "What? You can kiss me when I'm not well, but I can't do the same?"

Those lips parted in a tiny breathless gasp as Frankie gaped at me. "You remember that?"

I just nodded and watched as a bright flush illuminated his dark skin.

He slapped my uninjured shoulder.

"You didn't say anything about it, so I thought you forgot."

"No. I just didn't know what it meant."

Dark eyes glanced down at the lack of space between us and the arm I still had wrapped around him. "So, what does this mean now?"

I hadn't thought about it and didn't actually know what to say. So, I took a risk and spoke the words that were in my mind without hyper-analyzing them. "It means that you're upset, and I don't like it when you're upset. Someone like you deserves to only experience good things, and I want to be the one to give you those good things. Does that make sense?"

"You know..." He considered me for a moment. "It actually does."

Then he wrapped both arms around my neck and pulled me in for another kiss. This time, with both of us participating equally, the embrace was even deeper. He licked at my lips, his tongue beckoning me to come play with him. I was happy to oblige, and the minute my lips parted, his tongue immediately darted inside my mouth like it was determined to make a new home there.

We kissed until we couldn't breathe, then parted just enough to catch our breaths before melding back together. At one point, we lost our balance and tipped over. Frankie ended up lying on his back on the bed with me kneeling over him, but we never broke the kiss. If anything, it only heightened the passion growing between us and I practically crushed Frankie into the mattress as we desperately made out like teenagers.

When I finally pulled back and looked down at Frankie below me, the other man was a mess. With kiss-swollen lips, glazed eyes, and tangled braids that created a halo around him on the bed, he was deserving of a centerfold despite being fully clothed.

It was the first time I could remember that I didn't mind getting a little messy.

Unfortunately, with only one arm for support, I couldn't stay kneeling over him. So, I moved to lie beside him instead. He clung to me and buried his face against my chest, and I was happy to act as his pillow.

"Hey, do me a favor," he said without raising his head, so his vibrating voice tickled me through my shirt.

Now that I was no longer holding myself up, my hand instantly found the back of his head and I started stroking over his braids. "That's a dangerous agreement to make until I know what the favor is."

He finally looked up at me and fisted his hands in my shirt like he was afraid I'd disappear.

"You were right earlier. You can't stop doing your job, and I wouldn't want you to. However, when you go check out the place where Tansie Bell's son was seen, take me with you. I know I may not be as capable of a fighter as you, but I'm not useless. I can still help, and you need some support. You can't do everything alone."

I pressed a quick peck of a kiss to his lips, silencing him.

"All right. You can come."

His eyes lit up. "Really?"

"Yes, really. And don't ever say you're useless. Nothing could be farther from the truth."

CHAPTER FOURTEEN

Frankie

LEAVING THE SAFE house without taking the RV felt almost like cheating on a spouse. I had a strange urge to apologize to the RV for leaving it behind and I couldn't help glaring at the new car suspiciously. In contrast, however, it did feel good to not be the one responsible for driving.

Since the shootout with the FBI a few weeks ago, Gabe had managed to procure a different car, so we didn't have to take the RV every time, and now, he sat behind the wheel while I rode shotgun. I tried to keep the frown off my face whenever I looked at him, but it was impossible.

"Stop looking at me like that," Gabe said when he brought the car to a stop at a red light.

I reluctantly turned my gaze out the window. "I don't know what you're talking about."

Gabe let his gaze leave the road to give me a knowing look over the rim of his glasses. "I can feel you glaring at my arm."

"You're still injured." My voice was much softer than I intended, and my glare probably looked more like a pout. "You should still be wearing the sling to support your arm."

Although Gabe shook his head, there was a slight smile on his face. "It would be too noticeable. Besides, the exercises and stretching you have so diligently insisted I do have helped, and the worst of the internal damage is healed. A sturdy bandage under my shirt will suffice."

I was about to argue further when he leaned over and kissed me, which put an end to whatever I was going to say.

In fact, it put an end to any coherent thought for a while.

Damn.

For someone who seemed like such an ice-king on the outside, Gabe was a surprisingly good kisser. At this rate, I'd never win another argument now that he knew how to turn my brain to useless mush.

The sudden sound of a car horn made me jump, and even Gabe flinched a little. We'd been so preoccupied that we hadn't noticed the light turn green, and the drivers of the cars behind us were getting angry.

Gabe didn't even look embarrassed when he started driving again while my face was on fire. Forget the mafia, the corrupt Senator, and the pedophile ring. This man was going to be the death of me.

How was I supposed to live in close quarters with him for an unknown amount of time now that I knew he had this softer side to him?

Despite sleeping in the same bed every night, we hadn't done more than kiss, yet even that felt like too much for my nerves. Because of that, it was almost a relief to get out of the house.

Gabe had agreed to let me come with him when he investigated the location where Tansie Bell's son was spotted. It was a good chance to give Newt and Sebastian some privacy, something I knew they were desperately missing, and maybe even provide an opportunity to figure out where I stood with Gabe.

Assuming I ever worked up the courage to ask.

We arrived in Baton Rouge. It was the same city where I'd been living before all this started, and a place I hadn't expected to see any time soon. Yet, the fact that our investigation led us right back to the same place didn't surprise me. Baton Rouge was the capital, after all. Other than New Orleans, it was the most important city in the state.

Gabe found a place to park the car in an out of the way parking lot, and I stepped onto the city street with an odd surreal feeling.

Although it hadn't actually been that long since my peaceful life was interrupted, it felt like a lifetime ago, and even being back in the same area felt like stepping into an old outfit that no longer fit.

Like most cities in this part of Louisiana, there were a lot of rivers and bridges interrupting the streets. That was the consequence of building cities in an area with so much marshland and swamp. Water was an inevitable part of every citizen's life. Yet, after living in a house out in the woods, where I saw nothing but trees every day, I found my eyes no longer accustomed to the landscape I'd once considered home. I couldn't help watching the river as Gabe and I walked down the street toward the spot where Tansie Bell's son had been seen.

A sign for boat tours of the nearest swamp caught my attention.

"Hey, Gabe. You ever visit a swamp?"

He eyed me for a moment, probably wondering if there was a hidden meaning behind my strange question.

"Yes. A few times, though not recently."

I dodged around a few people on the street in order to stay at his side.

"I went on a swamp tour once for a middle school field trip when I was a kid. Tourists love them, so I was excited to see what all the hype was about." Recalling the memory, I shuddered. "I fell out of the boat right into a slimy patch of algae. I've hated swamps ever since."

A man talking on a cell phone as he walked tried to push between us. I was ready to step out of the way, but Gabe grabbed my wrist to keep me close. The man ended up bumping into us and looked up from his phone with an angry look on his face. His anger died the moment he realized how far he had to look up to meet Gabe's eyes, and he immediately shuffled away.

It was one of the benefits to being tall, I supposed. People naturally got out of his way.

That was a luxury I would never know. I wasn't the shortest person, especially not when I stood next to Newt, but I wasn't particularly tall either.

Gabe kept walking as if we'd never been interrupted, and the hand on my wrist slipped around my waist instead.

"Did you have any help falling out of the boat?"

So distracted by the casual way he embraced me, I almost missed his question.

When I realized what he meant, I gave an awkward laugh and scratched at the back of my head. "According to the official incident report, I fell on my own."

Gabe scowled down at me, but I had learned to read his expressions well enough to understand that he wasn't mad at me, but rather mad at the situation. All I could do was shrug.

"Middle school wasn't as bad as high school, but I still wasn't exactly popular." Gabe gave a little sound of acknowledgement, encouraging me to keep talking without saying a word. "Anyway, the point is that I hate swamps, and I've never understood why they attract so many tourists."

"People like experiencing things that are different from their normal life. And swamps are certainly a different than most people's everyday life."

"If they want to experience something new there are a thousand things I can think of that would be more pleasant than slimy water and alligators."

As we walked, Gabe started playing with my belt loop. It was such an automatic gesture, like his arm just belonged there around my waist, that it left me reeling.

We hadn't even slept together, yet Gabe was treating me as if we were already dating. Our first kiss had only been a few weeks ago, and before that I hadn't been sure Gabe even liked me. He really was a man of extremes, and I suspected he was the type to quickly commit once he decided on something.

We really needed to have a conversation about our expectations going forward, or this could get really messy.

I considered bringing it up right then, but before I could figure out how to start the conversation, Gabe announced that we'd arrived at our destination.

When reviewing a map of the area, we hadn't found anything that would justify why a pedophile ring would need to bring one of their victims here. The closest thing we could find to a point of interest was the office for the *Department of Wildlife and Fisheries*, which never seemed to actually be open based on their scant hours of operation. Other than that, there was a jewelry store, a few historical buildings, and several restaurants. All completely normal.

However, as soon as Gabe and I stepped onto the street in question, we were immediately brought to a halt by the sight of a familiar face.

Posters with Senator McLeod's image on them were plastered everywhere. Based on the information printed on the poster, it seemed the man was up for reelection, and was trying to advertise his best qualities.

So, of course, "Leader of a Pedophile Ring" was nowhere on the list.

"The timing of this is concerning," Gabe said as he inspected one of the nearest posters. "Although, I'm not sure what this would have to do with Miss Bell's son."

"Yeah." I narrowed my eyes at the Senator's printed grinning face. "If I were the leader of a pedophile ring running for reelection, I'd want as much space between those two parts of my life as possible."

At the front of the street, we came upon a booth that seemed to be the source of the posters. There were several people manning the booth, speaking with passersby about Senator McLeod's accomplishments, and handing out flyers to anyone who would take one.

Gabe seemed happy to watch the campaign efforts from afar, so I stepped up to the booth to see what information I could learn.

"Hello," one of the men running the booth greeted me.

The man's nametag said Ozias. It was an old-fashioned name for a young man, but I'd heard worse.

His face was just a little too plain to be handsome, but he had a boyish quality to his smile that could be called attractive.

"Are you interested in *Love Without Limits*?"

I tried to keep the suspicious look off my face. "I'm afraid I don't know what that is."

Rather than be put off by this, Ozias's eagerness only grew as he shoved several pamphlets toward me. "It's our new charity organization. *Love Without Limits* is Senator McLeod's newest effort to help the community. Its aim is to help women and children, especially those that come from disadvantaged situations. See, here."

He pointed to something in one of the pamphlets, but I didn't have time to read more than two words before he started talking again.

"Our first goal is to set up pop-up stands in major cities where expecting mothers can come for free health evaluations and prenatal care. There are also plans to eventually set up more affordable childcare services, as well as promote awareness for the needs of new mothers. It's a great cause."

"I see," I said absently as I scanned through the pamphlets. "And this is a new charity."

"Brand new, so we need all the help we can get. I can take down your information if you're interested in volunteering."

The man already had a pen and clipboard in his hands, poised and ready to write. For the sake of keeping the conversation going, I gave him a fake name and phone number, and prayed he wouldn't try calling the number before I was able to leave.

Ozias was still writing my information down when I decided to try another line of questions. "I actually know some people who might benefit from a charity like this. What should I tell them to do? Can they just show up at one of these pop-up stands, or do they need to apply to something?"

As soon as he finished writing, Ozias used the pen to point at another pamphlet. "Anyone can show up to the pop-up stands where they can speak with one of our volunteer healthcare workers. Well, not anyone. They would need to be either an expecting mother, or a mother with young children since those are the patients that the pop-up stands are for. However, if your friends need more specific services or supplies, then there are a few different things they can apply for. There's a general list right here, and you can find more detailed information on our website."

"Right." I waved the pamphlets in front of me as if showing them off. "Thanks for the info. I'll be sure to tell my friends about it. I know a few of them could definitely use the help."

"Great," the man smiled again, but this time it seemed distracted as he was already switching his attention to the next person. "We'll reach out to you with volunteer opportunities, and I hope we hear from your friends soon."

I stepped back from the booth and used my shorter height to my advantage in order to disappear among the crowd around the booth. I'd barely taken a few steps away when Gabe's hand snaked back around my waist and pulled me to the less crowded side of the street.

When I showed him the pamphlets and explained the new charity Senator McLeod had apparently started, a deep scowl furrowed Gabe's brow.

"This really isn't good."

"I know, right." I tried to keep my voice down despite the noise of the city, for fear of being overheard. "Like, this kind of charity would sound great if I didn't know about the guy's other interests. But for the leader of a pedophile ring to start a charity specifically focusing on mothers and children... Do you think this is some sort of cover for them to get their hands on new kids."

"Possibly." Gabe nodded as he looked up the charity's website on his phone. "It could be a way for them to find women interested in giving up their kid for adoption without the need to use hospital administrators."

"Could?" I studied his face for a moment and could practically see the wheels turning in his head. "You think it might be something else?"

"Look at the website. There is a bigger emphasis on mothers than children. If they just wanted to get their hands on more kids, then that's what they would focus on."

Gabe handed me his phone, where I quickly scrolled through the website's pages. "While there are services offered that help kids, there was definitely a much bigger focus on helping mothers. Specifically, disadvantaged ones, such as single mothers, and women from poorer income homes.

"So, you think they want to... what, find expecting mothers to kidnap instead of kids? Why? I can't believe I'm saying this, but why wait months for a kid to be born when you can steal one that's already born?"

When I looked up from the phone back at Gabe, I found him studying the sky with deep stress lines etched on his face. Taking off his glasses and storing them in his pocket, he rubbed tiredly at his eyes.

"Because stealing one kid gets you one kid. However, if you kidnap a pregnant woman that you already know is fertile, then you could have access to a lot more kids in the future."

"You mean, like..."

My brain came to a shuddering stop as

a single image filled my mind. I could see it so clearly, some young faceless woman imprisoned in a cell and forced to pop out kid after kid as sacrifices to the sick desires of her captors.

Bile rose in the back of my throat.

"I think I'm going to be sick."

Darting into an alley between two buildings, I braced my hands against the wall as I dry heaved. I didn't actually throw up, thankfully, but it was a close call.

When I was finally able to breathe properly, I realized Gabe was rubbing my back.

"I'm all right."

He passed me a water bottle. Where he'd gotten it, I had no idea, but I was too thirsty to care.

Maybe I'd been out of it longer than I thought for him to have time to buy it and come back.

I chugged half the bottle in one go, then slowly sipped on the other half as I waited for Gabe to say something. He never commented on my reaction, just silently watched the street and the people coming and going from the charity booth.

"You have a pensive look on your face,"

I eventually said once I'd finished the bottle and tossed it into a nearby trashcan. "What're you thinking?"

"I'm thinking that I'd really like to see the list of everyone who works for this so-called charity. And a list of the women who have applied for their services, while we're at it. See that van over there?" He nodded to a van parked in another alley on the other side of the street. "While we've been standing here, I've seen some people working the charity booth drop things off in there. Including the sheets where they write people's names down."

Thinking back to the fake name I gave Ozias, I realized he had written everything down with a pen and paper. I'd been too focused on other things to notice, but once I thought about it, I realized how odd that was. In the modern digital age, a pen and paper were usually a backup option, not the primary plan for keeping important information.

"Digital paper trails are harder to get rid of than literal ones," I suggested. "Maybe this is their way of ensuring that they can easily get rid of evidence if necessary."

"My thoughts exactly. If we could get

into that van, we might be able to get our hands on some of those lists.”

I studied the street. It was too crowded to break into the van without being seen.

A smile spread over my face, and I looked up at Gabe.

“Hey, Gabe. Can you create a distraction?”

CHAPTER FIFTEEN

Frankie

I STOOD IN an alley behind the office for the *Department of Wildlife and Fisheries* and peered around the corner at the van. No one was around it at the moment, but it sat right at the mouth of the alley. There was no way for me to get closer without being seen.

Instead, I stood waiting, and ducked back around the corner every time it looked like someone might be coming near the van.

About five minutes later, a car alarm started wailing. This wasn't unusual in a big city, but then another went off, and then another. Soon, at least a dozen cars that had been parked along the side of the road were all screaming in unison. I couldn't see the cars, but I could see the people on the street all stopping to stare in the same direction.

Specifically, everyone was looking in the opposite direction of the van.

This was my chance.

As quickly as I could, I crept closer to the van, and pulled out the pieces of wire I'd acquired earlier. Just like I had with the pharmacy when I needed to get medicine for Gabe, my fingers easily remembered how to maneuver the wire in the lock. The latch on the vehicle was even easier than the door to the pharmacy, and with only a few seconds of effort the back of the van was open for me.

Those car alarms weren't going to last long, so I didn't waste time and immediately started searching through the van. It was full of supplies, but most of it was innocuous. Stacks of printed flyers, all bearing the Senator's face. A tent to put over the booth, presumably to keep it dry if the weather turned and it decided to rain. There was even a box of streamers and balloons that someone must have decided at the last minute was too juvenile and was excluded from the charity booth's decorations.

None of it was what I was looking for.

A few of the car alarms went silent. The remaining ones still made plenty of noise, but I was running out of time.

I had to stop blindly searching and start thinking with a criminal mindset.

If I was trying to hide sensitive information in a place that wasn't easily found but also not incriminating, where would I hide it?

Well, I wouldn't be able to make any obvious alterations to the van. That would be too suspicious, and my plausible deniability would go out the window if the alteration was ever discovered. So, the lists would have to be hidden in a part of the van that would typically exist on this type of vehicle.

Snapping my fingers, I pushed a few stacks of flyers out of the way to reveal the latch for the spare tire compartment under the floorboards.

Locked.

Annoying, but a good sign that I was on the right track. Normal people didn't bother locking up their spare tire.

With the help of my homemade lock pick, I had the spare tire compartment open almost as quickly as I'd opened the van's door.

Jackpot.

There were several binders of paper stashed where the spare tire should have been, and a quick glance showed that they were full of lists of names. One binder looked to be lists of women who had applied for help from *Love Without Limits*, and another was filled with info about the charity's volunteer staff. The third binder I didn't recognize the information it contained, but I grabbed it anyway.

We needed all the info we could get, and I wasn't about to waste this opportunity.

I closed and relocked the van just as the last car alarm fell silent. With the binders clutched in my arms and turned to run from the van, only to immediately run smack into Gabe.

"Whoa. Oh, hey. You're back. Good job with that distraction."

He didn't say anything. Just grabbed my arm and quickly dragged me away from the van. We stuck to back alleys and didn't stop running until we'd put several blocks between us and the van. I wasn't even sure which building we were behind or which direction the car was, but it didn't matter. We were safe, and we'd gotten away with some hopefully useful information.

"That was fun," I gasped. It was hard to speak as I caught my breath while also trying not to laugh from the sheer exhilaration of it all.

Gabe wasn't laughing, nor was he even breathing hard, so his next words were crystal clear.

"You know how to pick locks?"

If I'd been paying attention, I would have noticed the odd tone in his voice. Instead, I just smiled up at him with a proud flush on my cheeks.

"Oh, yeah. I told you how I had a rough time after I was attacked and lost my scholarship. Well, I kinda went off the rails for a while. Nothing too bad but breaking into places became a common hobby for me. I didn't steal stuff. I just liked the thrill of being where I wasn't supposed to be and knowing that I could steal something if I wanted to. You know."

I held out the three stolen binders to him.

"My physical therapist helped me through it, and eventually, got me back on the right track, but I've still got the skills. Never thought I'd put those skills to good use like this, but, ta-da. Success. Hopefully, we'll be able to do something with these lists."

My excited flush turned to ice in my veins when I finally noticed the look on Gabe's face. He stared at the binders in my hands with an odd expression. It wasn't mad, but it certainly didn't look happy either. He was obviously feeling some sort of strong emotion, but I had no idea what it was.

"Sorry," I said, though I wasn't sure what I was apologizing for. "I just wanted to help, but I guess I shouldn't have—"

Before I could finish, I was suddenly shoved backward against the alley wall. Gabe's hand on the back of my head protected it from hitting the brick as he pressed his mouth to mine. I shouted into the kiss, uncertain what was happening at first, which provided an opening for his tongue to plunge forward. My shout turned into a moan, and I kissed him back with equally heated force.

I wanted to cling to him, but my hands were stuck gripping the binders that were now crushed between our bodies. Instead, all I could do was writhe in his embrace and try to spur him on with my enthusiasm.

He kissed me like he was trying to inhale me into his lungs while also surrounding me on all sides. It was midday. The sun shone high in the sky, yet Gabe's form blocked out the light and wrapped me in the coolness of his shadow.

There was no way to tell how long we stayed like that, but it must have been a while, because when Gabe finally pulled back enough for me to think straight, the angle of the sun had shifted.

My legs felt like someone had replaced my bones with jelly, but Gabe still looked infuriatingly composed as he started pulling me down the alley.

"Back to the car. We need to leave."

I obeyed automatically and followed him, despite the arousal still surging through me like an electrical current traveling from my brain to my toes and back.

Was that it?

The man practically sucked my soul out between my lips, then just moved on like nothing happened?

When we reached the car, I thought we might continue once we were safely inside, but no. Gabe started the engine and pulled the car onto the road without a word of explanation.

What did it even mean?

Was he happy about what I'd done?

Surely a kiss must indicate positive feelings. Yet, he'd walked away and continued as if nothing had happened. The man didn't even look flushed and not a hair stood out of place, while I felt like a throbbing mess of arousal and confusion.

Scowling, I tossed the binders into the backseat, then leaned against the window in the hope that the cool glass would calm the unsatisfied itch under my skin.

Not once, during the entire car ride back to the safe house, did Gabe look at me. He barely even said two words as his gaze remained locked on the road and his hands were perfectly poised on the steering wheel at ten and two.

I idly played with my braids, keeping my own hand busy. As I thought about it,

I came to two conclusions. Either Gabe hadn't agreed with my actions when I stole the binders and the kiss had been a way to shut me up and keep me obedient, or Gabe *did* agree with my actions, and the kiss had been his idea of a reward for a job well done. It certainly hadn't been due to any actual desire on his part. He'd walked away too easily, as if we'd merely exchanged handshakes.

Eventually, I settled on the second option. The kiss had been meant as some sort of reward for successfully stealing the binders. There were worse reasons to be kissed, but it wasn't the one I wanted. While the kiss had been hot during the moment, once it was done it felt like a business exchange.

Empty.

Cold.

Emotionless.

The hours back to the safe house were the longest, most awkward car ride of my life. We didn't even play the radio. Just sat in silence as the miles flew by under our tires.

When we reached the safe house, I wasn't sure whether to feel relieved or even more frustrated. Newt and Sebastian would break the unbearable silence, but I would have to act composed around them while on the inside I felt like a cat whose fur had been rubbed the wrong way.

Taking a deep breath, I stepped out of the car. The weather had been getting warmer recently, but the air within the shadow of the woods was still cool and refreshing in my lungs.

In the front window of the house, I could see Newt and Sebastian moving around in the kitchen. Newt seemed to be doing most of the work preparing something, but Sebastian was managing to help here and there from his wheelchair. It wasn't ideal. The size of the kitchen, and the house in general, made it difficult for Sebastian to maneuver the chair, but it was the most activity I'd seen from him since he was injured. No matter how frustrated I was in that moment, seeing one of my patients making good progress always brought a warm feeling to my chest.

I reached for the door handle to go inside, but Gabe's hand on my wrist pulled me away.

"Hey, wait. Where are we going?"

His only answer was to pull me toward

the RV, which sat exactly where I had left it. Although the sun was still in the sky, it was blocked by the foliage of the surrounding trees, so the atmosphere inside the RV was as dim as dusk. The door to the RV rattled on its hinges when Gabe closed it hard enough for me to feel the vibration through the floor.

When he finally let go of my wrist, I crossed my arms and scowled at him. "Are you going to explain what you're doing, or am I going to have to guess?"

I'd barely finished speaking when Gabe grabbed my face between his hands and kissed me. It was just as hot and intense as back in the alley, as if the several-hours-long car ride never happened and we were immediately picking up where we left off. The quick change between hot and cold and hot again left my head spinning.

"What is up with you?" I demanded when I managed to pull away enough to gasp out a few words.

"You just..." Gabe gripped my upper arms almost hard enough to bruise and he seemed to be fighting off the urge to shake me. "Do you have any idea what you do? What you cause?"

At first, I thought he was angry at me,

but that didn't align with the kiss. There were a lot of reasons to kiss someone, and anger wasn't usually one of them.

I looked at him closer. His gray eyes were dilated so wide his pupils had practically swallowed the iris.

With a snap of clarity, I understood.

"Oh." Reaching out, I plucked at the buttons of his shirt. "I see. My little act of petty theft got you all... flustered."

He shook his head but didn't let me go. If anything, he pulled me closer. "Not petty. And barely theft. That info could be used to hurt a lot of people, and now, we can protect them instead."

I wrapped my arms around his waist and pressed close enough to feel his arousal through his pants. "So, that's what does it for you? Getting to be the protector?"

This time, when he pressed his lips to mine, there was an added growl of frustration at the back of his throat. He nipped my bottom lip, adding a thrilling bit of pain to the pleasure.

"That's not it. Many people would help in that situation, but they would hesitate to put themselves in danger. You didn't hesitate. You never do."

Smirking to myself, I pushed him away so there was more space between us, conveniently moving myself closer to the bed at the back of the RV.

"Some people would call that reckless."

Just as I hoped, Gabe followed me.

"Reckless. Yes." He grabbed onto me, his hands wrapping around my waist, but he kept walking so I had no choice but to back up until my knees hit the side of the bed. "Also infuriating, arousing, and confusing."

He found my neck with his lips and pressed a line of warm, biting kisses from my ear down to be collarbone.

"I never know what to do with you."

He slipped his leg between mine, so his thigh pressed against my groin. The unexpected stimulation made me flinch. I stumbled backward and fell onto the bed in an artless display of sprawling limbs. The mattress cushioned my fall, so nothing hurt, but the unexpectedness of it all left me breathless nonetheless,

As I looked up at Gabe from where I lay on the bed, I waited for him to join me. Yet, in an odd reaction, he closed his eyes and tipped his face toward the ceiling instead. Running his hands over his hair to smooth it back into place, he seemed to be counting silently under his breath.

I swung my legs around and clambered onto my knees to get a closer look at him.

"Are you… doing breathing exercises to calm yourself down right now?"

He opened his eyes, and his pupils no longer looked as dilated as they had before. "Apologies. I was getting too worked up."

My mouth hung open as I gaped at him with a comical expression. "Worked up? I certainly hope so. If there's any time to get worked up, this is it. Why do you say that like it's a bad thing?"

A slight blush turned his earlobes red. It was a subtle color, but on Gabe's usually stoic face, subtle reactions were the same as screaming.

"I tend to… forget myself when I get worked up. I'm told that I can be too much, so it's better if I stay calm."

"Oh, no. Fuck that." I found the button of Gabe's pants with shaking fingers and fumbled it open. "This is not the time to stay calm. I'd prefer *too much* than *not enough*." A thought occurred to me as I started unzipping his fly. "Is this why you suddenly stopped kissing me back in the alley? You were afraid of getting too *worked up*?"

Gabe gripped my wrist, though he didn't stop me as I slowly slid his pants over his hips. "The alley wasn't safe."

He was too distracted by what I was doing to explain further, but I knew him well enough by now to read between the lines.

"You didn't think you'd be able to stop if we went any further back then. Fine. But you could have just told me that."

His pants landed on the floor in a puddle around his feet, and I slipped my hand inside his underwear.

"You left me hanging for hours, horny and confused, with no explanation. I had to sit through that whole car ride wondering what I'd done wrong." I wrapped my fingers around the very hard shaft of his cock, gripping him tightly, and then I looked up at him through my eyelashes. "Make it up to me."

I could see in his eyes the moment that his control snapped, though I didn't have time to revel in my victory. He grabbed my shoulders and shoved me onto my back on the bed. His weight pinned me down when he lay over me, gripping my wrists in both hands as he brought his mouth down on mine once more.

CHAPTER SIXTEEN

Gabe

THE FEELING OF Frankie pinned under me was even better than I imagined. I wouldn't lie, I had dreamed about such a thing several times since our first kiss, and even before that, but the reality ended up being so much better.

He was warm and pliant in a way I hadn't been prepared for. Given his indomitable personality, I expected him to push back when I pinned him down. For him to remain obstinate even in an intimate moment such as this. Yet, the minute my weight settled on top of him, he fell still in a way I'd never seen before.

As if he were finally comfortable for the first time.

Maybe what he said was true. I hadn't been giving him enough. I'd been so concerned with staying in control of myself and not holding on too tightly that I had accidentally not held on tight enough.

At least not in the ways that mattered.

I'd tried to protect him, even to the point of almost controlling him, but I hadn't made it clear that I wanted him.

Well, if giving into my baser desires was what it would take to make him happy, I could do that.

Without breaking the kiss, I started tugging at his clothes. He moaned against my lips and tried to help but couldn't do much in his position. I ended up doing most of the work removing our clothes, but I didn't mind. In fact, it was a thrilling experience getting to handle him how I wished.

Soon, but not soon enough, he lay completely bare to my eye. I'd moved us to the center of the bed, so his head was properly cradled by the pillows. He lay there, hands up by his shoulders and his legs partially open, in a position of complete vulnerability. He let me see everything about him, and it made me want to hide him away so no one else could ever look at him again.

Instead, I knelt between his legs and rested my hands on his knees.

"Beautiful."

He blushed and turned his head to hide his face against his shoulder.

"No," I said with a stern tone. "Don't hide. Keep looking at me." I gripped his chin and tipped his head to face me.

He squirmed and nodded but didn't try to remove my hand.

"Good. Just keep looking at me." The praise fell from my lips much easier than words usually did just before I leaned in and kissed him again.

Without our clothing, there was nothing stopping me from feeling every inch of him. He was just as aroused as I was, and he whimpered into the kiss as our hips ground together.

I left his mouth to travel down his neck instead. I latched onto a spot that made him squirm, right at the juncture where his neck and shoulder met, and sucked until his flesh turned hot under my lips. The mark left behind was barely visible on his dark complexion, like a secret hidden in plain sight.

Farther down, I used my teeth and tongue to trace patterns over his chest. He was lean, but still soft around the edges, and the muscles of his chest had just the right amount of give when I squeezed them.

He seemed to enjoy the rougher handling and grabbed my shoulders to pull me closer.

I flinched when his fingers dug into my injured shoulder. The bullet wound was much better than it had been a few weeks ago, but still not completely healed.

Frankie, of course, immediately noticed my reaction and jerked his hands away like he'd been burned.

"Sorry. I forgot. Are you okay?"

I laughed softly and moved farther down to lavish attention on his stomach.

"It's fine. More shock than actual pain."

Each word was punctuated with a nip to the sensitive flesh of his stomach. His whole body seemed to quiver with every application of my teeth against his flesh. Although he nodded as if he understood what I'd said, he still burrowed his hands under the pillows by his head like he didn't trust himself to touch me now.

I didn't mind. With his arms out of the way, his body was left on full display.

Moving down his stomach, I was so close to the prize between his legs that my breath ghosted over his cock. He moaned and squirmed just from the promise of stimulation, and when I pulled away, he actually wailed in despair.

"What? No. Why'd you stop?"

Leaning over to the drawer beside the bed, I pulled out the supplies hidden there.

Frankie stared in confusion at the box of condoms and lubricant I tossed beside him on the bed.

"Where did those come from? I don't remember buying that when I was at the store."

I couldn't even bring myself to feel embarrassed when I admitted that I'd bought the supplies after we kissed the first time. It had been a moment of hopeful thinking that was definitely paying off now.

Frankie nodded, but his lips were pursed. "And why were you hiding this stuff in the RV?"

The answer seemed so obvious I was surprised he needed to ask.

"Where else would I keep it? If we did end up being intimate, the RV would provide more privacy."

He laughed and threw one arm over his eyes. "You really do like to plan ahead. Don't you?"

"Of course."

With his arm over his eyes, he couldn't see me. I took advantage and quickly repositioned myself to take his cock into my mouth. He shouted in surprise from the unexpected stimulation and tried to buck his hips, but I held him down against the mattress.

"Fuck. Warn a guy."

His words lacked heat when he could barely speak them around his constant moaning.

I'd never been good enough at oral sex to figure out how to swallow someone completely. My gag reflex only let me take about half of Frankie's arousal into my mouth, but he seemed to be enjoying it anyway. Especially, when I ran my tongue along underside of the head.

At the same time, I fumbled for the bottle of lubricant sitting only a few inches away. When I finally managed to get it open, I coated two of my fingers in the clear substance. Then, without ever stopping the motion of my mouth, I prodded my fingers between the lush globes of his ass.

This time Frankie couldn't even form words. His moans merely took on a frantic edge and he kicked his heels against the mattress as I slipped one of my fingers inside him.

He was tight, but obviously experienced enough to know how to relax and let me in. I didn't have to wait long before my second finger was able to join the first, and I set to work plunging my digits deep inside him. As I continued to lavish attention on his dripping cock, I also searched for the sweet spot that would make everything a hundred times more enjoyable for him.

"Fuck. Gabe. Keep going." He twisted his hands so tightly in the pillows I was surprised he didn't rip them.

As much as I enjoyed hearing his voice, the command was unneeded. I had no intention of stopping.

I knew I'd found the right spot when he suddenly arched his back and pushed his cock deeper into my mouth. I nearly choked but managed to pull back just in time. To make up for it, I kept rubbing at that spot inside him until he was half crazed from the constant stimulation.

His climax was quickly approaching, if his tightly pulled up sack and the loud responses were any indication. If I kept going, he'd soon tip over that edge of pleasure. I wasn't ready for that to happen just yet, though. I pushed him as far as I dared, but before he could find his release, I stopped and removed my fingers from his heat all together.

"Bastard," he snarled at me. "Don't you dare stop now."

In response to his demand, I grabbed his hips and flipped him over, so he lay on his stomach. I could hear him muttering curses against the pillows, but he didn't protest or try to stop me as I positioned him with his shoulders against the mattress and his hips in the air. It was such an inviting position, I shuddered, my cock throbbing in anticipation just from the sight of Frankie spread open and waiting for me.

Quickly rolling a condom onto my hard as steel shaft, I knelt behind him and lined up with his eager fluttering hole.

It was a lucky coincidence that one of my favorite positions also allowed me to sit up straight and keep my weight off my injured shoulder. There would be nothing to stop me from giving Frankie everything I had.

The other man growled against the pillows when I stopped to savor the moment. "Would you hurry up. Bastard. You're trying to kill me. I swear."

Who was I to deny such an order?

Gripping his hips in both hands to hold him steady, I shoved my dick inside him with one long, smooth thrust.

The feeling of him tightening his muscles around my cock was more perfect than I could describe. It stirred something primal within me that I usually kept locked away.

I wanted to claim him.

Own him.

Engrave myself so deeply into him that he could never find satisfaction with anyone else.

Frankie's groans and begging words were only a distant echo in my ears. As soon as I'd seated myself all the way inside, I grasped his hips tighter and pulled out again. I barely left any time for him to adjust before I started fucking him at a punishing pace. He babbled something against the pillows, but he wasn't making any sounds of pain, and he never asked me to stop.

That was all the encouragement I needed.

My vision blurred around the edges and tunneled until all I could see was the way Frankie's whole body jolted each time I drove my hardness inside his sweet ass. Pleasure danced through my veins, but it was soft and mellow. The sharp edge that signaled an approaching orgasm was missing, and I knew from experience it wouldn't show up for a long time.

In contrast, Frankie seemed to already be riding the edge of his own pleasure. I couldn't see his face, but I could tell from the way the muscles in his back tensed and he squeezed even tighter around my cock that his release was rapidly approaching.

It probably didn't help that I was hitting his sweet spot with each thrust, but I had no intention of stopping.

When he fell over that blissful cliff of his orgasm, he buried his face against the pillow to muffle his scream. His whole body became a vice grip around me, and his inner muscles fluttered so frantically it almost felt like he'd started to vibrate.

I never stopped or slowed down, riding him through his orgasm until he was openly sobbing and clawing at the mattress.

When it finally ended, he fell limp in my grip and gasped for air. His muscles twitched and shuddered like he'd just run a marathon.

In response to his sudden lethargy, I started plunging into him harder, taking his hole for my pleasure like I owned it.

"Fuck," Frankie shouted which I hit his sweet spot again. "You're like a damn machine."

Since he'd just come, his nerves must have been so over-stimulated. Every time I thrust inside him, it probably sent a confusing mix of pleasure and pain rushing through him. I could tell from the way he kept trying to pull away and push closer at the same time.

I groaned low under my breath and sped up, keeping a tight grip on his hips to ensure he wouldn't be able to escape me for even a moment.

He started begging, but even he didn't seem to know what he was asking for. It was just a constant stream of, "Please. Too much. I can't. Don't. So good. Too much."

I basked in the sound of his desperate voice and kept my steady pace.

Eventually, my persistence won, and his cock grew hard again. It wasn't as desperate as his arousal had been before, and bobbed lazily between his legs like it couldn't make up its mind.

Without halting my movements for even a moment, I reached around him and started stroking his hardness in time with my thrusts.

"No," he moaned long and low, while at the same time practically humping my hand. "Don't. I can't. Too much."

He came again, this time accompanied by the sound of ripping fabric. He'd torn one of the pillows under his clawing hands and spread tufts of cotton all over the mattress like snow.

I sped up. Seeing him so desperate pushed me another step toward my own end, though I still wasn't there yet.

His second orgasm finished, and he was well on his way to a third when I finally felt the pleasure in my gut tighten and my balls pull up with a telltale signal that I was close.

By this point, Frankie had fallen quiet, his body easily accepting me each time I filled him. Even his breathing had slowed like he was in some sort of trance, though every now and then a pitiful little whimper escaped his lips.

When he reached his peak a third time, I managed to follow him. I clamped my hands down on his hips, my nails punishing his skin and leaving crescent-shaped indents, and I pushed myself as deep inside him as I could. His inner muscles clenched around me, milking the orgasm from me, and dragging my pleasure out even longer.

For how long it took me to reach climax, it also took me a long time to finish. The ecstasy rolled over me in waves, one after the other, and every time I thought it was done, another would hit.

Several minutes must have passed before I finally came crashing down from my peak. I felt worn out, and I wanted to just collapse on the mattress, but I had to take care of Frankie first.

Pulling out of him slowly, I disposed of

the condom in a nearby trash can and helped him lie flat on his back. Then I headed for the RV's minimal bathroom and grabbed a wet washcloth in order to clean up the other man.

I was wiping down his inner thigh, careful not to touch any areas that looked too sensitive, when Frankie finally came back to his senses.

"What the fuck was that?"

My heart sank. The few times I'd been comfortable enough to share a bed with someone in the past, it always ended this way.

"Sorry," I said as I set the washcloth aside. "As I said, I've been told before that I'm too much."

"Too much?" Frankie repeated as he stared up at the ceiling with dazed eyes. "I'll say. You're way too much, you jackhammering terminator. I thought you were going to break me."

As I tried to repeat my apology and even promise to never touch him again, he grabbed my arm and pulled me closer.

"Do it again."

"What?"

He tugged at my arm until I had no choice but to lie beside him. "You're right.

You are absolutely overwhelming. Do it again." He shifted on the mattress like he intended to roll toward me, but then grimaced and lay still. "Although maybe not right now. I'm dead. You killed me. But soon, definitely do it again."

Breathing a sigh of relief that I hadn't just ruined my relationship with the beautiful man, I helped Frankie roll over, so his head lay against my chest like a pillow.

Frankie yawned, and I felt his warm breath brush against my skin.

"Do you think Newt and Sebastian realize we're out here?"

Through the RV window, I could just see part of the safe house. Dusk had fallen while we'd been busy, and the lights glowing from inside the house looked warm and inviting.

"Probably. But I don't think they'll be too surprised."

CHAPTER SEVENTEEN

Gabe

SEBASTIAN'S LEG WAS finally healed enough to get him a new, more manageable cast.

Supposedly.

Without an x-ray to check how his bones were healing, there was no way for us to know for certain. Unfortunately, an x-ray was one form of medical care that couldn't be provided at the safe house by Newt or Frankie. We needed a hospital with proper medical machines.

It took some effort, but with Lily's help, I managed to get an appointment set up in a hospital far enough away from the safe house that our enemies would not easily be able to track us.

"Thanks again, Lily," I said into my phone as I sat in the hospital's waiting room. "I wouldn't have been able to set this up without you."

"Eh, this was nothing," her voice floated through the phone. "I wish all my jobs were this easy. Those lists of names you sent me are proving trickier than I thought."

"The lists we got from the Senator's new charity? What's so complicated about that?"

In the seat beside me, Frankie perked up and strained to listen to my conversation. He must have been able to hear enough to realize what we were talking about, but not enough to get the full detail though, because he looked confused. If we were in private, I would have put the phone on speaker so we could both listen, but the hospital waiting room was too public. Someone could overhear, so I just signaled that I would tell him later.

In the background of the phone call, I could hear Lily's pen tapping against her desk. "Well, the first two binders were exactly what you thought. There was a list of women who have used *Love Without Limits's* services, and a list of volunteers who work for the charity. I've got people investigating those names right now. However, the third binder I can't figure out. It's a list of names, addresses, and phone numbers like the other two, but none of these people actually exist. My bet is that they are either aliases, or it's some sort of code. I'll let you know when I figure it out."

I nodded, trying to keep the disappointment from showing on my face. "All right. If anyone can figure it out, it's you. Is that it?"

Although I couldn't see her, I could hear the laughter in her voice. "Would I leave you with just that? Have a little more faith."

I sat up straighter in my chair. "You've got something?"

"Two things that'll interest you. First, that guy you spoke with who was manning the charity booth. His full name is Ozias Wren. It's a unique name, and it sounded familiar, so I dug a little deeper into him. Mr. Wren has been a busy little volunteer helper, specifically this last year. Wanna guess where else his name popped up?"

I didn't need to guess. Just from her tone, I could already tell.

"One of the hospitals where children went missing?"

"Several of them, actually. The man has been all over the state of Louisiana, and even a few other states. I'd say he's either a part of this pedophile ring, or at least working for them."

Since my phone was occupied, and I didn't trust myself enough to start hitting buttons without accidentally hanging up on Lily, I pulled out a notepad from my pocket and wrote down the name Ozias Wren as well as any details I could remember about the man. Lily would undoubtedly send me the man's file later, but there was something about writing with pen and paper that felt more productive.

"Okay. That's one lead we can look into. You said there was a second thing I'd want to hear?"

"Yep. I saved the best for last. *Love Without Limits* is having a big charity event soon. The Senator's even going to show up. That would be a perfect time for you to do a little snooping."

"I'll mark it on my calendar. Thanks again. I'll keep you updated on how it goes."

"Not a problem. Helping you is certainly better than dealing with the chaos going on here since the Director was killed. Did you know some people are suggesting that I take over as Director? I said absolutely not and threatened to quit on the spot."

I made sure to keep my laughter at a reasonable level for a waiting room, though a few people nearby still gave me odd looks.

At my side, Frankie was practically bursting at the seams with curiosity.

"You'd be a miserable Director."

"I know," she groaned. "I'd much rather be the woman behind the power. I've got to go now. Give my regards to Mr. Roth. I hope his injuries are doing better."

After saying goodbye, I hung up the phone and turned to Frankie, expecting to be bombarded with questions. However, rather than immediately ask about the new information I'd learned, Frankie started with a completely unexpected question.

"What's the relationship between you two? You seem to trust this Lily woman implicitly even though she works for the FBI, who have recently tried to kill you and accused you of being a mole."

I studied Frankie's face for a moment and was relieved not to find any hint of jealousy or suspicion. My relationship with him was still new. We'd only been sleeping together for a few weeks—I refused to count exactly how many because I didn't want to put a quantifiable number on something that felt so natural—so there was still plenty of room for miscommunication.

Being with Frankie felt too good. I refused to let it corrode over something as illogical as jealousy.

"She was friends with my sister, Ariel."

At first, I was going to leave it at that. The simple explanation would be enough to satisfy Frankie's curiosity. However, I realized I didn't want to hide the truth from the other man, not even through omission. I wanted Frankie to know my full story. Even the unpleasant parts.

"The two of them used to hang out all the time. Then, one day, they were out having lunch when Ariel suddenly stopped breathing. She died before the ambulance even got there. The official medical report said it was an allergic reaction to something in the food, but that's a damn lie. My sister didn't have any allergies."

I pulled my glasses out of my pocket and fiddled with the arms as I considered putting them on. I really only needed them for things like driving and reading, but they added an extra shield between me and the world that I could hide behind.

In the end, I tucked them back into my pocket and faced Frankie without any barrier between us.

"Lily had just become the Director's secretary then. I'm certain someone tried to kill her and accidentally poisoned Ariel in the process. I don't blame her, of course. I blame the person who killed my sister."

Frankie's slipped his hand into mine and laced our fingers together. "Who killed her?"

I narrowed my eyes, the anger washing through me even just thinking about the name.

"David Russo. He wanted Lily to be his spy in the agency, and when she refused, he tried to have her killed. I could never prove it. Lily helped me get a job in the FBI so we could look into it together, but even the two of us weren't able to find the necessary evidence. The case is too cold, now. I don't think we'll ever prove it. However, there's no doubt in my mind. That bastard killed my sister."

The feeling of Frankie's head leaning against my shoulder was a pleasant weight. Especially, since it was my injured shoulder, yet I felt no pain. The wound was almost completely healed.

"No wonder you were so eager to help Sebastian and Damien," Frankie said. "They're victims of the head of the Mariano family, too."

I squeezed Frankie's hand tighter, though I was careful not to grip too tight.

"That monster has left too many victims in his wake. One day, I'll see him dead."

Anything else I would have said on the matter was cut short when I caught sight of Newt stepping through the door into the waiting room. Behind him, Sebastian followed a moment later, still in his wheelchair.

At first, I was filled with excitement and relief. Sebastian's full-leg cast had been removed and replaced with a smaller cast that only covered the bottom part of his leg. It was the same kind of cast he'd been walking around in right before the bomb went off in the apartment and put him on an even more difficult healing journey.

Surely, that must mean that he was ready to walk again.

A doctor also accompanied the pair and seemed to be explaining something to Newt as they walked. As a nurse, Newt kept a professional expression on his face as he listened to the doctor, however, Sebastian was a different matter.

"Ah, fuck," Frankie hissed at my side.

I stayed silent but agreed with the sentiment.

The sour expression on Sebastian's face told me everything I needed to know. The prognosis for his leg wasn't good.

CHAPTER EIGHTEEN

Frankie

THE PROGNOSIS COULD have been worse. Sebastian's leg had accepted the various pins holding it together and started knitting the bones back together around them. Everything structural within the leg seemed to be aligned properly and it should be able to bear some weight by now, with the help of a partial cast.

The problem came with actual movement. Sebastian's leg didn't seem to want to move, and when it did, the movements were sporadic and uncontrolled. I suspected damage within the muscles, perhaps even deeper nerve damage, but such things were hard to diagnose with one hundred percent certainty.

All we could do was wait and work with the leg to get it moving again. Only time would tell if the limb could be retrained for more control, or if it would remain partially paralyzed.

Our first goal was to get Sebastian standing again. With the help of Gabe and Newt, we set up a pair of support bars for Sebastian to hold onto while he practiced putting weight on the leg. Several different pairs of crutches sat stacked in a corner of the safe house, like a hopeful reminder, but Sebastian hadn't even glanced their way since returning from the hospital.

"Keep your weight on your legs even," I reminded Sebastian when I noticed him leaning slightly to one side. "You need to train your leg to move properly. If you get in the habit of favoring one leg over the other, then your leg will learn that motion and you'll have to retrain yourself later."

Sebastian grit his teeth so it looked like he was snarling at me. "If I don't rely more on my good leg then I can't stand for long." His voice came out growly and labored, betraying the effort it took the man to stand.

I crossed my arms and stared him down with the most unimpressed look I could manage. "Then you don't stand for very long. I'd rather you stand for one minute properly than five minutes lopsided."

Luckily, we'd tested the bars several times before trusting them to support Sebastian, even going so far as to have Gabe, Newt, and myself all hanging on them at once. If they weren't so secure, they probably would have collapsed from how hard Sebastian's arms shook as he struggled to hold himself up. At least seventy-five percent of his weight was being supported by his arms, yet even that was a challenge for his leg.

It had only been a few days since we returned from the hospital, yet it seemed Sebastian had expected to be able to immediately start walking again. The fact that he couldn't do so was obviously frustrating the man, but we had to be patient. Healing such a devastating injury took time, and it was going to be an even longer journey if Sebastian was already fed up. He needed to stay positive and keep working slowly, but for a man of action, such gradual progress was unbearable.

At Sebastian's current strength, he could only work for about an hour before he needed a break. I let Newt tend to him by fetching him water and a snack and massaging the muscles in his leg to keep them from cramping up.

Meanwhile, I sought out Gabe, who was hiding in our bedroom. He was on the phone talking to someone with a serious look on his face, so I closed the door quickly behind me.

"I know you're worried," he was saying as I sat next to him. "I've looked into it and have some leads to follow. When I've got more concrete information, I'll let you know."

I placed my hand on his knee in a silent question.

He blocked the phone with his hand and spoke so quietly that he was basically just mouthing the words. "Miss Bell."

For a moment, it looked like he was going to say more, but his attention suddenly snapped back to his phone. "What do you mean?" Whatever Tansie Bell said was too quiet for me to hear, but a shadow fell over Gabe's face. "No, don't. If you see anything else, don't engage on your own. Send me what you have, and I'll look into it."

The rest of the conversation mostly consisted of half sentences from Gabe that I couldn't follow. All I could tell was that he seemed to be talking Miss Bell out of doing something.

I waited for the conversation to end before I asked what was going on, but it turned out I didn't need to. The minute Gabe hung up the phone, he let out a harsh sigh and then told me everything on his own.

Apparently, Miss Bell had been patrolling the streets of Baton Rouge, searching for any sign of her son, and she'd just caught another glimpse of the boy.

Gabe pinched the bridge of his nose like he was getting a headache. "It's lucky that the boy disappeared inside a locked building before she could approach, otherwise she would have made a target out of herself just like us. Although this does confirm our suspicions. The area where the boy was seen is near where the Senator's charity fundraising event is going to be held. We definitely need to attend the event, though I have no idea what the boy is doing there in the first place."

I absently rubbed my hand along Gabe's arm in a show of support. Under his shirtsleeve, I could feel the raised edges of his scars like tiger stripes. In the chaos of everything happening, I'd never asked about them. My curiosity was piqued but there were bigger things to worry about.

"We'll figure it out," I said, even as I never stopped my hand movements. "First, we need to prepare for this charity event. When is it again?"

Gabe told me the date and I ran through a calendar in my mind. We had some time before the event, but not enough.

"Sebastian is insisting on coming, but I don't know if he'll be healed enough by then."

I hadn't even finished my sentence before Gabe was shaking his head. "If he's not healed enough, then he should stay here where he is safe. We don't need another liability to look after."

Groaning, I flopped back on the bed. "I

know, but try telling him that. Especially, since Newt is insisting on coming to the event as well, and I don't think we can afford to turn him down. The two of us alone may not be enough to cover the entire event and keep an eye on everything. There's no way we'll convince Sebastian to stay behind if Newt comes."

The mattress shifted as Gabe leaned over to plant a hand on either side of my shoulders, so he was kneeling over me.

"Maybe we can find a compromise that'll keep him happy."

My laughter came out as more of a snort. "Compromise? You? Since when do you even know that word?"

"Perhaps you've been rubbing off on me."

I had a joke all lined up about "rubbing off," but I never got the chance to say it.

Gabe kissed me hard enough to press my head back into the mattress. I responded by pulling him closer and wrapping my arms around his neck. He slid his hands over me, pushing my shirt up and my pants down to reveal as much skin as possible.

I tried to do the same, but our position

didn't allow us to undress very well. Aside from opening a few buttons, we remained mostly clothed.

I'd never been with a man who liked kissing as much as Gabe did. All of my previous partners treated it as a necessary step on the way to what they actually wanted, like putting coins into a vending machine. If they put enough intimacy in, then they eventually got sex in exchange.

It never really bothered me until I met Gabe, but now that I knew what it was like being with a man who actually enjoyed the intimate side of sex, I wouldn't settle for anything less.

Was I spoiled for any other man?

Probably.

Was I going to consider what that meant for my future love life?

Not right now.

Maybe, once everything else was settled and we were safe and no longer in hiding, then I could think about it. For now, I was just going to enjoy being alive and take advantage of the few pleasures my situation brought me.

Eventually, Gabe grew impatient, and he sat up so he could properly divest me of my clothes. I let him, but only because I was too busy trying to remove his at the same time. In the end, all of our clothing ended up in a scattered pile over the floor. I could see the slight twitch in Gabe's eye as he was struck by the urge to properly fold our clothes, but after weeks of sleeping together, I'd gotten better about distracting him.

I lay back on the bed, my body on full display, and ran my leg over his hip.

"Come on. You're not going to leave me waiting like this? Are you?"

I thought Gabe would come closer and let me wrap my arms around him again. So, I wasn't prepared for the cold rush of air that hit me when he stood up. Without the heat of his body, I shivered against the sheets and couldn't control the whine that slipped past my lips.

"No. Come back."

I reached out desperately for him, but all he did was laugh at me with a smug little grin on his otherwise stoic face.

"Impatient thing, aren't you?"

I sat up so I could reach him. "Yes. Now, come here."

"No." With one hand, he pushed me back onto the bed. "Stay there. The only thing you need to do is concentrate on staying quiet."

Before I could ask what he meant, I yelped when he suddenly knelt at the end of the bed, perfectly positioned right between my legs. I had just enough time to clamp my hands over my mouth and silence myself before he took my cock into his mouth.

Damn, the man seemed to have gotten better at controlling his gag-reflex. There was no hesitation this time before he swallowed me almost all the way to the root. The intense pleasure that surged through me was too overwhelming. My own hands clamped over my mouth were the only things keeping me quiet, otherwise, I definitely would have been shouting.

Sebastian and Newt were just in the other room. They would hear if we made any noise. While they probably wouldn't mind—the fact that Gabe and I were sleeping together was no secret—I wasn't into exhibitionism. The noises I made during sex were for only me and my partner to hear.

It took all of my concentration to keep my hands over my mouth and not make a sound. My whole body trembled with the effort.

Gabe, on the other hand, seemed to take it as a challenge. He did everything he could to make me lose control, alternating the movement of his head between quick and slow and using his hands to stroke lightly over the sensitive skin of my inner thighs. All the things he knew drove me crazy.

I squeezed my eyes closed and dug my fingers into my cheeks, completely ignoring the fact I might bruise my skin with how hard I pressed my hands over my mouth. The need to moan and make noise welled up in me, like water filling up behind a dam. I would burst eventually. Even the best self-control had limits, and mine was hardly the best, but I refused to give up so easily.

With his mouth and hands, Gabe drove me right to the edge of pleasure, but before I could tip over, he suddenly stopped. I nearly broke, and a low groan managed to escape past the iron grip I had over my mouth.

"Shhh," Gabe scolded me, letting his breath tease over my aching arousal.

I squirmed but didn't say a word.

After a minute, when my breathing had calmed down a little, he swallowed me again and picked up right where he'd left off.

"Bastard," I hissed through clenched teeth, though I barely removed my hands enough to speak, so I wasn't sure he heard me.

Through the tears of frustration that had gathered in my eyes, I looked down the length of my own body at him to find him looking up at me.

He'd definitely heard me.

I would have said more, but the sight of him staring at me with a smug glint in his eyes even as his mouth continued to pleasure me was surprisingly erotic.

A new wave of arousal washed through me, and I shivered. My stomach felt weak, and I couldn't continue to hold myself up enough to keep looking at him. I collapsed back on the bed, my head thrown back as I stared up at the ceiling and kept my hands firmly locked over my mouth.

There was no telling how long that went on, though I could hear the ticking of a clock somewhere in the distance beyond the wet wounds Gabe was making. Over and over again, he'd bring me right to the edge of orgasm, then stop before I could finish, only to start again after I'd calmed down. The man could have kept edging me like that forever and I wouldn't have complained, but denying me also meant denying himself, and even Gabe's iron will had a limit.

I could tell when his patience began to run out. He started to growl low in the back of his throat like he was angry, sending the vibrations right up my aching cock and into my brain. I thrashed my legs, and he gripped my thighs hard enough to leave bruises, the thought of which only ramped up my arousal more.

His movements sped up, pushed me toward my end faster than before. For a moment, I thought he would finally let me finish this time, but I was wrong. Just as the pleasure started to tighten in my stomach and I was literally seconds from orgasm, he stopped again, and then pulled away from me completely.

I let my hands fall away from my mouth. "You fucker," I gasped, though I didn't have the energy to speak more than a whisper.

Somewhere in my peripheral vision, I noticed Gabe pulling out a condom, but I didn't bother paying attention until he was literally spreading my legs and shoving his fingers inside me. It was a quick and rough preparation. We were both too eager to wait much longer.

The moment I was deemed ready for him, he grabbed my legs behind my knees and lined himself up with my hungry hole.

The whole bed shook from the force of his thrust as he sheathed himself inside me, and I quickly covered my mouth again to stifle my moan.

His thrusts came hard and fast, and I trembled as I lay there and took the pounding. I couldn't even wrap my legs around him since he kept his hands hooked behind my knees.

After being kept on edge for so long, it was no surprise that I came quickly. It was also no surprise that Gabe didn't even slow down as I shivered and whined through my orgasm, coating my belly in my own hot spend. During these last few weeks together, I'd gotten used to the man's endless stamina. More than that, actually. I might even say I loved it. There was something erotic about being taken so relentlessly, abandoning all hesitation, that satisfied a deep primal urge.

I really was spoiled for any other man. It was probably too early in our relationship to make such declarations, but I could no longer picture myself with any man other than Gabe. Somehow, in such a short amount of time, I'd become addicted to him.

Just like every other time we'd been together, Gabe took a while to reach the edge of his own pleasure. He was ruthless in his pursuit, claiming me over and over again until he'd completely wrung every drop of pleasure from me. Yet even then he kept going.

Before Gabe, I'd never experienced a dry orgasm before. To be struck with the electric thrill of climax, yet produce nothing to show for it, was an odd sensation the first few times it happened. However, I'd quickly grown used to it. I now even looked forward to it. It was an overwhelming type of pleasure that I only experienced with Gabe, like a signature he left branded on every inch of my skin.

I knew when Gabe was close, because he suddenly started thrusting harder and faster, chasing that edge that was just out of reach. My muscles twitched from over-stimulation, milking him each time he drove deep into me.

Unlike me, he didn't make a sound, even when he came. His eyes became glassy, and a flicker of several different emotions danced over his face all at once. Even after my own pleasure faded, the urge to moan remained until Gabe finished as well. I didn't dare release my hands from my mouth until we'd both calmed down.

Gabe separated us carefully and handled the clean up like usual. I'd tried to help before, but he always insisted. He seemed to treat it as a ritual, like he was slowly adjusting himself from the haze of sex back into reality.

I didn't mind. It meant I got to lounge around and be taken care of. I'd never considered myself a pillow princess before, but Gabe was quickly turning me into one.

We lay together on the bed as the afternoon sun shone through the window. We were still on top of the sheets, but I wasn't cold as Gabe lay overtop of me. His head was on my stomach, and his arms casually draped around my waist like I was a pillow or a stuffed animal for him to snuggle.

I watched the sunlight dance on the ceiling each time the wind blew through the trees outside, and idly ran my hands through his hair and over his shoulders.

My fingers found the raised edge of the highest scar on his left arm, and I was reminded of my question from earlier. Tracing the scars one by one, I debated if I should ask or not.

Was it the right time?

Would it ruin the mood?

In the end, I decided to ask. If we had reached the point where I couldn't imagine myself with any other man, then we needed to keep an open line of communication between us and not shy away from difficult questions.

"How did you get these scars?"

I waited for his reaction. To my relief, he looked up at me with mischief in his iron gray eyes.

"You're a physical therapist. How do you think I got them?"

I studied the scars more closely, although I didn't actually need to. I knew exactly what they looked like and had already run through the many options in my head.

"At first, I thought they were knife wounds, based on their long slashing shapes, but they aren't quite smooth enough. Some of them have ragged edges, and don't follow the line that a knife would. Plus, they all seem to be the same age, so unless you were attacked by Edward Scissorhands, getting that many knife wounds in one place at the same time seems unlikely."

I couldn't reach all of the scars on his left arm from where I was laying, and I didn't want to get up, so I started back at the top, near his shoulder, and started tracing them again.

The glimmer left Gabe's eyes as he listened to my deduction process, but his expression was still warm.

"Whenever people ask, I tell them I was attacked by a lion."

"And they believe you?"

"You don't?"

I shook my head and one of my braids fell across my neck like a choker. "They aren't clustered together enough to be claw marks. Despite working in the city, I've seen a surprising number of patients who have been attacked by wild animals to know what those look like. I didn't know that bears could live in swamps, but apparently they can, and people are dumb enough to try and approach them."

This time, Gabe didn't say anything as he waited for my final verdict.

"Shrapnel," I eventually declared. "Probably razor blades, or something equally sharp. You probably weren't too close to the bomb when it went off, since there are no burn scars, but the shrapnel still reached you."

Laughing quietly under his breath, Gabe buried his face against my stomach.

"I shouldn't be surprised," he said against my skin. "You are good at what you do." He looked up at me again with a complicated expression. "My last mission with the Army Rangers, an IED went off and nearly took my arm with it. If I'd been any closer, I would have lost the limb, and it took several years of physical therapy to get a full range of movement again. Ended my active military career."

He fell silent for a moment, and I could see him weighing different words in his mind. His gaze darted side to side, like he was reading the sentences as he considered them before speaking.

I would have been satisfied with that

answer, but I left it up to him if he wanted to tell me anymore.

Eventually, after several minutes of silent debate, he found his voice again.

"I should have seen the IED before it went off. Looking back on it now, it was obvious, but I was distracted."

"Distracted?" One disbelieving eyebrow journeyed to the top of my forehead. "Since when are you ever distracted?"

"I was distracted that day. I'd just gotten a message... I told you about how my sister died, right? Well, that was the day I was told about her death. I shouldn't have been out in the field after getting that kind of news, but we were in enemy territory. We couldn't just turn around and go home, even if we wanted to. I thought I could hold it together, but I wasn't paying as much attention to my surroundings as I should have been. This is the result."

I left his scars behind to wrap my arms around him instead. "I'm sorry. To hear that kind of news about your sister, and then immediately get injured, it must have been horrible."

He slipped his hands under me so he could wrap them around my waist. "It was. I won't say it wasn't. For years, I hated the sight of the scars, but now, they're a reminder."

"A reminder of your sister?"

Gabe shook his head and let his chin rest on my stomach as he looked up at me. "A reminder to hold on tight to the things I care about."

Moisture gathered in my eyes, and a knot in my throat kept me from speaking, but I didn't need to. All I needed was to hold him close as his arms wrapped tighter around me and bask in the feeling of safety that he brought.

We lay there for several hours until Newt knocked on our door to announce that dinner was ready. There was a lot to do. My stomach was growling, Sebastian would need another round of physical therapy before the end of the day, and we still had preparations to make in order to investigate the upcoming charity event.

However, I used that moment to hold Gabe close just a little longer, clutching each other tightly until our fingers left identical bruises behind.

CHAPTER NINETEEN

Frankie

THE CHARITY FUNDRAISING event turned out to be an indoor carnival. Usually, carnivals were an outdoor event, but the spring weather was still too cold and wet to allow such a thing. One might wonder why the event would take the form of a carnival at all if the weather didn't allow for it. Surely, there were plenty of other types of events that could be used to raise money.

As I stood at the center of it all, looking around at the various rides and attractions, I knew exactly why a carnival had been chosen and my heart sank at the sight of every smiling face. Carnivals catered to families and children. It provided plenty of opportunities for the Senator's "people" to scope out new victims.

"This place is making my skin scrawl," I whispered to Newt, who stood at my side as the two of us pretended to watch a juggling act.

Gabe had managed to land a spot among the event's volunteer staff. It gave him a perfect opportunity to unearth anything suspicious about the event, but I hated the idea of him being on his own. He felt too vulnerable to me, although Newt and I were probably the ones more at risk as we played the role of visitors. If we ended up having to fight our way out of a dangerous situation, we wouldn't fare nearly as well as the ex-military man.

If only Sebastian had been able to come, but despite my efforts with his physical therapy, he hadn't been healed enough. Instead, we'd found a compromise. Sebastian stayed in the RV, which was parked just a few blocks from the carnival, and watched everything through a pair of pins that Newt and I wore that each held a small camera and a

GABE

GPS tracker.

I had no idea where Gabe had gotten hold of the pins, but I suspected Lily was probably involved.

Occasionally, Sebastian texted us to point out things he'd noticed through the cameras. The man was, unsurprisingly, very observant. He had a good eye for just where to stand to get the best view of every attraction, and pointed out suspicious characters in the crowd long before Newt and I even noticed them.

It would be much easier if we actually knew what we were looking for. The instructions to look for "anything suspicious" weren't specific enough. So far, our efforts had helped us catch two pickpockets, and a pair of teenagers making out behind the popcorn stand.

That last one was embarrassing for everyone involved, and not the least bit helpful.

We'd been at the carnival for a few hours, and walked by all of the attractions at least once, when I noticed something familiar. At first, I didn't know what I was seeing, but my subconscious was waving a red warning flag at me, which was definitely worth investigating.

I led Newt toward the back corner of the indoor carnival, near the wall that was painted black and draped in dark fabric to give the illusion of more space.

The larger attractions, such as funhouses and roller coasters, were stationed at the back of the building since they attracted the most people. Newt and I had to push our way through the crowd, but I eventually found what had caught my attention.

Ozias Wren.

The man I'd met at the charity's information booth a few weeks ago, and if Lily's information was accurate, a likely member of the pedophile ring we were hunting.

At least, I thought it was him. I only saw him for a moment before he stepped inside one of the funhouses. He was dressed in clown makeup, as many of the people working at the carnival were, so I couldn't be certain of his identity. I needed to get a closer look.

"Newt, come on. Let's go in there."

"Are you sure?" Newt eyed the funhouse skeptically. "What would we even do if we caught up to him? He hasn't done anything. At least, nothing we can prove. Won't following him be suspicious?"

"What? No. This is a public event." I led Newt toward the funhouse. "And we're just two members of the public that have come to enjoy ourselves."

Through the front entrance of the funhouse, which was shaped like a giant ice cream cone, we stepped into a world of swirling colors and shapes. The whole thing had a candy theme, like a cheap knockoff of Willy Wonka's factory.

Newt and I stood out a lot more than I expected. Some parents had brought their kids inside, but most simply allowed their kids to run around alone. The contained structure of the funhouse probably assured parents that their kids couldn't run off or get into trouble.

As the only adults without kids, we looked out of place.

"Let's just find the guy and see what he's up to. If he's not doing anything bad, then we can leave."

That was a lie, and Newt and I both knew it. There was no way we would be comfortable leaving a member of a pedophile ring alone with so many children, even if he wasn't actually doing anything right that moment.

Stumbling our way through a spinning tunnel and a hall of mirrors, we eventually found the man we were looking for at the funhouse exit. There were two ways out of the building. A spiral staircase, or a slide. There was a man stationed at the entrance to the slide, helping each kid get situated before they went down.

I watched for a moment, making sure the man was who I thought he was.

Yes, it was definitely Ozias Wren. What I had originally mistaken for a clown costume, was actually a harlequin. He wore a pair of checkered pants, a diamond printed waistcoat, and a matching mask that covered half his face. There was also a surprising amount of jewelry to go with the costume, including several layers of necklaces, and rings on most of his fingers.

The overall effect made him hard to identify. If I hadn't gotten a good up-close look at the man before, I wouldn't have recognized him at all.

Each time Ozias placed a hand on a kid's shoulder or waist as a way of helping them, a little more bile built in the back of my throat.

Yet, there was nothing we could do. Helping the kids was his job, and he wasn't doing anything wrong. Whatever sick thoughts might be going through his head at that moment weren't technically illegal.

"Are you going down?"

I jumped when Ozias addressed me directly. I'd been staring at him so long—probably glaring—that I hadn't realized I'd gained his attention.

He didn't say anything about Newt and I being the only adults present without kids, but just held out a hand toward the front of the slide.

"There are stairs, but this is definitely the more fun way down. Come on. Give it a try."

Newt and I shared a brief look. We could decline and take the stairs, but it would definitely look suspicious.

Why else would a pair of adults come into the funhouse without kids if we weren't even going to participate in the attraction?

"All right," Newt said, and he stepped up to the slide.

I clenched my fists behind my back as

I watched Ozias take Newt's hand and help him sit down, and I didn't breathe again until my friend disappeared down the tunnel.

Then it was my turn.

I avoided Ozias's hand when he held it out to me and sat myself on the edge of the slide. Yet, the man still placed a hand on my shoulder, just low enough that I could feel the cool touch of one of his rings against my skin.

I shivered and pushed myself down the slide as quickly as I could to get away.

The slide was a twisted tube that went from dark to light and back again, like a very slow strobe effect. It would have been fun under a different context, but at that moment I just wanted it to be done.

Newt was waiting for me at the bottom of the tube, brushing dirt off the back of his pants where he seemed to have landed on the ground.

"Well, that was pointless."

I shrugged and climbed out of the mouth of the tube.

"At least we know it's actually him. Maybe there's a way to get the guy fired from the carnival. Could we maybe frame him for something?"

GABE

"Hold on." Newt sat down on a nearby bench and pulled out his phone. "I'll ask Sebastian about it."

His fingers flew over the keys as he typed out a quick message. With nothing better to do, I leaned against the bench and watched each kid that came out of the slide.

They seemed all right. None of them showed any signs of distress, but what was I expecting?

Big black handprints on their bodies to show if the man's hands had wandered to inappropriate places?

"Sebastian says not to do anything to confront Ozias," Newt reported after a moment of back and forth texts. "We'd only draw attention to ourselves. He's going to see if Gabe can do anything to at least get the guy reassigned to a different part of the carnival where he won't be in such direct contact with kids."

"Better than nothing I suppose."

Newt tucked his phone back into his pocket, and a flash of red caught my eye.

"Hey, Newt. Are you bleeding?"

Surprised by my sudden question, Newt held up his arm to reveal a single drop of blood running down his wrist to his elbow.

"Oh, I guess I am. Did I scratch myself on the slide? Weird. I didn't feel anything."

He wiped the blood away with a tissue to reveal the tiniest pinprick on his wrist, almost too small to see. For such a small wound to bleed that much, it must have been deep.

I stood up from the bench, intending to inspect the odd wound closer. Yet, the moment my weight settled on my feet I staggered.

"Frankie, you all right?" Newt shouted when my knee hit the ground. He stood, reaching out to help me, but he stumbled as well.

"What the hell..." My speech was slurred.

What was going on?

The image of Ozias's hand gripping Newt's wrist flashed through my mind. Following a sudden hunch, I craned my head to the side to look at my shoulder.

A drop of blood rolled down my arm, starting just under the sleeve of my shirt, where Ozias had touched my skin.

"We need to go. Now."

I grabbed Newt and tried to stand, but

my vision wobbled, and I fell over again.

To my side, Newt was having the same problem. He braced his hands against the ground to keep himself upright, but I could already tell it was a losing battle.

I pulled my phone from my pocket to try and tell Gabe what was going on, but my fingers were numb. The device slipped from my grip before I was even able to turn it on.

"Hey, are you all right?" someone asked.

I couldn't see who spoke. Everything around me was blurring together, and I couldn't even tell which direction was up and down.

The last thing I heard before I passed out was an unknown voice calling for the carnival staff to come help.

CHAPTER TWENTY

Frankie

THE GROUND BENEATH me rocked as I woke up. My cheek pressed against something hard.

Since when was the bed, I shared with Gabe so uncomfortable?

I groaned and tried to roll away, but I hit another solid surface. This wasn't Gabe. The man was muscular, but even he wasn't so literally unyielding.

Memories came back to me in a rush.

The carnival.

Ozias Wren.

A drop of blood running down Newt's wrist.

My head shot up, but the rest of my body didn't follow. I was lying on the floor of... something. I couldn't see enough to tell what. It wasn't a car, but it was definitely moving. I could hear the sound of wind blowing just above my head, and the smell of wet vegetation hung so thick in the air I could taste it on my tongue.

Like rotten salad.

Turning my head to the side, familiar orange hair filled my vision and provided a measure of relief. At least we hadn't been separated.

"Newt." I reached for him but found I couldn't move my arms. They were bound behind my back at an uncomfortable angle.

Desperately trying not to panic, I nudged Newt with my leg instead. "Hey. Newt. Wake up."

"Give your friend a break. That's a hard drug to shake off."

I jumped at the unexpected sound of a familiar voice.

"Ozias?"

A pair of boots stepped into view, stopping just inches in front of my face, before the man knelt down close enough for me to see him.

"You know me? Diligent little investigators, aren't you? Well, I should thank you. If you hadn't shown up, I would have had to wait a lot longer."

From my position bound on the floor I couldn't really glare up at the man, but I tried anyway. "Wait for what?"

Grabbing me by the back of my shirt, Ozias hauled me off the floor. The collar of my shirt dug into my throat, cutting off my air until I was placed sitting up with my back against a wall. Finally, I was able to get a good look at my surroundings, and my heart sank so low it reached my feet.

A swamp.

We were in a swamp.

Of all the places they could have taken us, why did it have to be a swamp?

Goosebumps prickled my skin just from the smell. There was no sign of civilization anywhere, and there was no telling where we were exactly. Louisiana was rich with swampland, and our small boat seemed to be right in the middle of a particularly remote patch of wilderness.

I curled my legs close to my chest. "Why are we here? What do you want with us?"

Ozias perched on the edge of the boat with one leg crossed over the other like he was lounging on a park bench. "Oh, I don't actually want anything from you. You're nothing to me. But, capturing you did earn me enough favor to gain access to the island."

I looked around again at our surroundings. Tall trees grew straight out of the murky water and the vines hung down from their branches in such thick clumps they looked like ragged curtains. In the daytime it may not have been too bad, but at night the shadows clung to every surface, and the boat's small light barely allowed us to see a few feet in any direction.

"Why would you want to come here?"

The man's grin made my skin crawl.

"So, I can have my pick of the dolls."

Dolls?

That had to be a euphemism for something.

Was he referring to the missing children?

He had to be.

What else would a member of a pedophile ring get so excited about?

That meant the children were here in

the swamp somewhere, and this man captured Newt and I so that he could come here to…

My brain refused to finish that thought.

"You fucking pedo."

I kicked him, striking as hard as I could with my unbound legs.

He flailed for balance and almost fell over the side of the boat but managed to catch himself at the last second.

I wished he had fallen over. Even if he didn't drown, it would have at least made me feel better. The disgruntled look on his face was still enough to make me laugh.

Rather than retaliate, as I expected, Ozias just crossed his arms and scowled.

"You're going to regret that."

Before he'd even finished speaking, a set of large hands picked me up and held me in the air so my feet didn't even touch the floor. I'd been so focused on Ozias, and the swamp around us, that I never noticed the other man in the boat. He was huge. A mountain of flesh, with a face that looked like it had been carved from rock.

The man who held me didn't say a word as he brought me to the side of the boat and bent me over the edge. His hand was so large it encircled the entire back of my head, and easily pushed my face under the water.

Still a bit groggy from whatever I'd been drugged with, it took me a moment to realize what was happening. When I did, I thrashed against the hands holding me. I strained against the ropes that bound my arms, and I kicked my feet against the floor of the boat, but it did nothing. The hands of the man holding me down didn't even budge.

My lungs screamed for air. The instinct to open my mouth was strong, and I bit the inside of my cheek as I fought the urge. If I opened my mouth, I would only inhale the disgusting water and drown faster.

After what seemed like hours, the hand holding my head finally let go and I was pulled back up into the boat. Despite my best efforts, I'd still swallowed some water, and coughed desperately to clear my lungs as I lay on the floor of the boat.

Through my struggles to regain my breath, I could hear Ozias berating the other man.

"Hey, don't kill him. I worked too hard

to capture these bastards. I'm not losing my ticket to the island because some meathead like you can't control his temper."

Pond scum dripped from my hair, and I shook my head to get the water out of my eyes. I wanted to retaliate and put on a brave face. I wanted to be like the hero of a movie who laughed at the villain's pitiful attempts at threatening them. However, I was also terrified of being shoved under the water and feeling that burn in my lungs again as my air slowly ran out.

Instead, I stayed quiet and inched over toward Newt. My friend seemed to be slowly waking up, and I didn't want him to panic. I positioned myself so I was the first thing he saw when he opened his eyes.

"Hey, shhhh. Don't make a sound. We don't want to get their attention."

Blue eyes looked at me in fear as Newt quickly took stock of our situation, but he listened to me and didn't say anything. I gave him a rushed explanation of what was going on, speaking mostly under my breath so our captors wouldn't hear me.

"We're gonna get through this, okay.

We just need to stick together and stay calm."

Newt swallowed a few times and nodded. "The pins."

I frowned at such a seemingly out of place comment.

"The pins we were wearing," Newt explained further. His eyes flickered over to Ozias and the other man before looking back at me with a pointed expression.

He didn't want to give away too much, but I finally understood what he was saying. When we'd been kidnapped, we'd been wearing GPS pins with cameras in them so Sebastian could see everything we were doing. The pins were gone now, probably removed while we were unconscious, but Sebastian would have seen us being taken. That meant he and Gabe were already looking for us. We just had to survive long enough for them to find us.

A little bravery returned to my soul. I imagined a ticking clock counting down each second until Gabe and Sebastian arrived. All we had to do was outlast the clock. It wouldn't be easy, but at least the goal was simple.

Newt and I kept to ourselves and tried

not to draw any more attention while we were on the boat. We sailed into the heart of the swamp, much deeper than any commercial tour would have taken us.

At least another half hour passed before we came across a structure among the trees.

The building was surprisingly modern for its surroundings. A low squat design with a small upper floor, it had been built right on its own platform to compensate for the lack of stable ground. It was not the kind of place where anyone would usually choose to build anything, right in the heart of a massive swamp, but it was the perfect area for something that needed to remain a secret.

Newt's shoulder bumped mine when he leaned over to whisper in my ear. "This land is completely wild. It's probably preserved. How is there a building here?"

"The same way these things always work. If you line the right person's pockets, you can get away with anything."

The boat pulled into an empty spot in the building's expansive dock. Knowing the purpose of the building, I was glad to see the dock mostly empty, but hated the fact that they needed such a large dock in the first place.

Upon arriving at the dock, however, we ran into a problem. Or, more accurately, Ozias ran into a problem. The person in charge of the building's security wouldn't let Ozias off the boat, and the two got into an argument.

"We had a deal," Ozias shouted, gesticulating so wildly that he rocked the boat.

The security officer didn't look impressed and kept one hand positioned on their impressively large gun.

"The deal was for you to help us capture either the Roth brothers or Agent Long. We have no use for their little whores."

Ozias was a surprisingly brave individual and didn't back down despite facing someone so heavily armed. "No, the deal was that I bring you something useful and I'm allowed on the island to have my pick of the selection here. Well, these two are useful. You can use them to lure out at least one of the Roth brothers, and that FBI agent. I've held up my part of the deal, now give me what I'm due."

The argument went back and forth for a few minutes but was eventually ended when the security officer received instructions from someone on his radio.

"Fine, you can come onto the island. But you're meeting with the boss first. If he decides these two are worth something, then you'll get your payment."

Several pairs of hands dragged Newt and I off the boat. No one listened to our protests or even seemed to notice our struggles. We may as well have been bags of flour being hauled from one place to another.

I'd never felt so powerless. Not even when we had to make a mad escape from the hospital. At least back then there had been something we could do. There were actions we could take to try and solve our situation. Now, there was nothing. Newt and I were being marched at gunpoint to face the very man in charge of all our recent suffering. Even if we could free ourselves from our ropes, we wouldn't make it two steps before we were gunned down. These people had already made it clear that we meant nothing to them. The only reason we were alive is that we weren't worth killing yet.

Inside the building, we passed the entrance to a long hallway on our way to the stairs. The brief look I got down the hallway showed rows of doors on either side, all heavily reinforced. It was like a perverse mix between a hotel and a prison.

I didn't count the doors. I didn't want to know how many children were probably locked away behind them.

Just the sight of the hallway made me want to scream, and I picked up my steps to hurry away from it. However, I was stopped abruptly when I ran straight into Ozias, who stood staring down the hallway with eager eyes.

"Keep moving," someone said, and shoved Ozias with the butt of their gun. "You haven't earned anything yet."

I gnashed my teeth, savoring the idea of tearing out the man's jugular any way I could.

Or maybe chop off his hands. Yeah, that was a satisfying idea.

Imagining everything I would do to the man if I could helped to keep me calm as we were marched away from the hallway and up the stairs.

The second floor of the building was much smaller than the bottom, consisting of just a few rooms. Newt and I were deposited inside a large office and left sprawled on the floor like a pair of broken toys.

It was a miracle I managed to land on my shoulder and not on my face.

Struggling to sit up without the use of my arms, I first noticed a couch on the far side of the office. The large piece of furniture dwarfed its only occupant. A young boy lay asleep on the couch, curled up on one end in a tight ball like he wanted to try and wrap his arms around himself as many times as possible.

There were bruises on his wrist and he looked too thin for his size. Only a small portion of his face was visible over the cushion he slept on, but it was enough to identify him.

It was Tansie Bell's son.

I couldn't look at the boy for long and turned my head away. This brought me face-to-face with the stout desk that took up the majority of the room, and the man sitting behind it.

Senator McLeod.

CHAPTER TWENTY-ONE

Gabe

"WHAT ARE YOU doing here?"

I stared, bewildered, at the woman who stood before me.

When I managed to get myself into a position as a member of the volunteer staff for the charity fundraising carnival, I thought the worst part would be working with the public, or possibly being recognized by our enemies.

Being approached by a familiar face was not one of my expectations.

"What?" Tansie Bell said as she looked around herself, as if searching for a reason for my question. "It wasn't hard to figure out. I first saw my son in an area where they were promoting this new *Love Without Limits* charity. Then I saw him again near the area where this fundraising event was taking place. Of course I suspected this charity might be involved somehow."

"No, I understand that," I said, rubbing my eyes under my glasses to try and relieve the tension headache that was growing in my skull. "But why did you come here? If the charity is connected to your son's disappearance, then coming here could be dangerous for you."

Luckily, the first-aid station where I'd been assigned was currently empty. So far, I hadn't seen anything worse than a few scraped knees, and one man who threw up due to the combination of fried food and roller coasters.

That meant that there was no one to interrupt me as I tried to convince Miss Bell to leave.

She planted her hands on her hips and stared me down. "I'm not going anywhere. If my son is here then I'm going to find him, with or without your help."

"All right. All right." I grabbed her arm before she could leave the first-aid station. "You can stay, but you have to do what I say. I don't think your son is here right now, but we may be able to find out about the people who took him."

Miss Bell nervously tugged at one of her thick braids. "Is that why you're working here? What do we need to do?"

I readjusted my glasses, taking a moment to resign myself to involving another civilian in such a dangerous situation.

"There is something you can do. I need to get into the event coordinator's office to take a look at their records, but it'll be noticeable if I leave the first-aid station unmanned. Cover things here while I get into the office."

At first Miss Bell looked eager, but once she realized what I was asking her to do, she looked around the first-aid station with trepidation. "But I'm not a nurse. I've never even taken a first-aid course."

I slipped off my glasses and stored them in a pocket of my jacket for safekeeping. "So far, there hasn't been any major injuries or anything that couldn't be solved with a band-aid or an antacid. It'll only be for a few minutes. I shouldn't be gone long."

Clenching her fists in front of her like she was preparing for a fight, Miss Bell nodded at me.

"All right. I'll do it. And getting a look at the event's records will help find my son?"

"Money always talks. Their financials will definitely help us figure out what is going on."

Once Miss Bell was settled, I left the first-aid station and headed for the offices at the back of the building. An outdoor carnival would have been preferred. Outdoor events usually had pop-up offices, which were little more than shipping containers dropped in the middle of a field and were much easier to break into. An indoor carnival meant a proper building and proper offices, with much more efficient security.

My volunteer staff shirt helped. Most people didn't give me a second look, but I ran into some trouble with the office door. The lock was surprisingly complex and took me a few minutes to force it open. It had been years since I learned how to pick a lock, and I hadn't used the skill very often. Both the Army and the FBI would usually just brute force any door open that stood in their way.

I realized I could have actually have used Frankie's help at that moment. The other man had a surprising gift for convincing locks to open for him. A talent I never would have suspected when I first met him, but fully appreciated.

The door eventually opened, and I was relieved to find there was no alarm waiting to be disarmed. However, I still couldn't afford to take my time. My position as a volunteer staff member allowed me to walk around the backrooms of the building unhindered, but I'd have no good excuse if I was caught in the manager's private office.

Along with the GPS camera pins that Newt and Frankie wore, Lily had also managed to procure us one more useful item. Computers were not one of my specialties, so I appreciated the small device that automatically copied the information of whatever computer it was plugged into.

It looked like an ordinary USB drive, and a red light started blinking when I plugged it into the office's only computer. I assumed that meant it was doing something and took a look around the rest of the office while I waited for the device to do its job.

Nothing. The office was surprisingly bare. There were a few folders stored in a filing cabinet that held time schedules for the carnival's various attractions, and a picture of a happy family sat on the desk, but otherwise, the office held nothing interesting. There wasn't even a safe or a locked drawer. Everything except for the information on the computer lay out in the open.

The device finished its job, indicated by the red light changing green. I grabbed it and left the office, relocking the door behind me with a frown on my face. It felt too easy. I should be happy that something was finally going smoothly, but after everything we'd been through so far, the lack of interference made me suspicious.

No one even stopped me in the halls as I made my way out of the back rooms and returned to the first-aid station.

Miss Bell looked up from where she was placing a band-aid on a kid's elbow. "Did you get it?"

I nodded but didn't say anything more in front of the kid or the kid's parents.

They probably weren't spies, but I didn't want to involve any more civilians if I didn't have to.

Three was already too many, and Sebastian almost counted as a civilian as well.

The first-aid station had a computer, but I didn't trust it. Instead, I'd brought my own laptop, which I propped up on the first-aid station's desk and used to look through the information I'd just copied. It all looked fairly standard. A lot of money needed to change hands in order to coordinate an event of this size, and it was no surprise that Senator McLeod was heavily involved in the exchange. The numbers added up, and I couldn't see any funds being used somewhere they shouldn't.

If I presented this to the FBI, any case against the Senator would be dismissed immediately. I was sure there was a metaphorical smoking gun somewhere that implicated his crimes, but it wasn't in these files.

As I scrolled through the information again, an unexpected name caught my eye. I hadn't noticed it at first because it wasn't suspicious or dangerous in any way, but it was odd.

Why would the *Louisiana Department of Wildlife* and Fisheries be involved in this event?

Even if *Love Without Limits* was a legitimate charity with no shady purposes, it should have nothing to do with a government department that handled wildlife conservation.

Before I could contemplate the odd discovery anymore, I was distracted by the sound of my phone ringing. The only people who had this number were Sebastian, Newt, and Frankie.

I picked it up immediately.

"Is something wrong?"

Sebastian immediately started shouting at me from the other end of the line. I could barely make out what he was saying, but the sound of Newt and Frankie's names were unmistakable.

"Did something happen to them? Where are they?"

Silence echoed down the line for a moment as Sebastian struggled to compose himself and speak properly.

"They're gone."

I stood up from the desk, knocking over my chair, which crashed to the ground in a noisy clatter. "What do you mean they're gone?"

"I mean, they're gone. Someone took them. I couldn't tell on the cameras, but I think they were drugged. Someone was shouting to get the event staff for help, and then the cameras cut out. I tried to track the GPS signal, but it's gone."

The laptop and the information I'd just copied were forgotten as I ran for the door.

"How long ago? Where were they last?"

Maybe if I ran fast enough, I could catch their kidnappers before they disappeared.

Sebastian directed me toward the candy-themed funhouse in the back corner of the carnival, almost as far from the first-aid station as it was possible to be.

When I got there, I found a group of people standing around talking excitedly, but no sign of Frankie or Newt.

"Excuse me. What happened here?"

Although my words were polite, there was no mistaking the demanding tone of my voice. The nearest man took one look at my staff shirt and glared at me.

"Some boys got sick. The staff already

took them to the first-aid station. Shouldn't you be taking care of them there or do you people not talk to each other."

Ordinarily, I would never tolerate such an attitude, but I had more important things to worry about.

Newt and Frankie obviously weren't brought to the first-aid station. I would have seen them. So whatever staff members took them away must have been working for our enemies.

I followed the path I thought kidnappers might take. First, they probably would have gone in the direction of the first-aid station to avoid suspicion. However, they would have needed to get Newt and Frankie out of sight as soon as possible. The funhouse itself would have provided the perfect cover. It was large and bulky, with many flashing lights and colors to act as a distraction. Even carrying two unconscious bodies, it wouldn't have taken much effort to slip behind the funhouse and out of sight.

From there, the path the kidnappers would have taken may as well have been marked in neon paint for how obvious it was. A door hidden at the very back of the event space led to a cargo bay, where the building would usually receive supply trucks. It was empty at the moment, but the open cargo door and the smell of gasoline indicated that a vehicle had just left.

I was too late.

As I stood in the open doorway, something hard and cold pressed against the back of my skull. I lifted my hands slowly in a show of surrender.

I knew a gun barrel when I felt one.

CHAPTER TWENTY-TWO

Frankie

I CLENCHED MY fists so tightly within their ropes that the tips of my fingers went numb. Senator McLeod sat at the desk in front of us, looking down on us as we knelt on the floor where we'd been dumped. A pair of armed bodyguards stood around him as Ozias carefully approached the desk.

"I did as you asked, sir. I brought you something useful."

Senator McLeod regarded Ozias for a moment, heavy brows furrowed, and fingers balanced like a steeple in front of him.

"I'll decide what's useful."

His chair creaked when he stood. The armed bodyguards moved with him as he approached, always at his back like a choreographed dance.

Beside me, I could feel Newt tremble.

The Senator grabbed Newt's chin and forced him to look up.

"Prettier than I thought they'd be. Our clients might even like this one. Despite his age, he's still got an innocent look to him."

Newt shook harder.

I snarled and pictured sinking my teeth into the man's wrist to remove his disgusting touch from my friend. With my hands bound it was all I could do, even in my imagination.

Yet, my silent threat only made the Senator laugh. He let go of Newt to grab my hair instead, and then tipped my head back as far as it would go. He brushed his fingers over the scar on the back of my head and I shivered with revulsion. Other than Newt, Gabe was the only person who I had allowed to touch that painful memory written on my skin. I hated how it felt, but was at least glad to have the Senator's attention as it meant the man was no longer paying attention to Newt.

The Senator was right. Newt's personality and wide blue eyes would be just the kind of thing these monsters would enjoy destroying.

As if sensing my thoughts, the Senator smiled and leaned closer until I could feel his breath on my face.

"This one's too feisty, but I know others with my exotic taste who would pay good money for him."

I was just considering the merits of spitting in his face—if the momentary satisfaction be worth the pain it would probably cause me later—when the Senator thankfully let me go and turned back to face Ozias.

"We can definitely profit off of them, but that's not my main concern. You're certain that they'll work as hostages for our targets?"

"Oh, yes," Ozias said, standing stiff as a board like a soldier presented before his drill sergeant. "Sebastian Roth will do anything for the redhead. And the FBI agent who's been protecting him seems to be fond of the other one. I've seen them together before."

"Good." Senator McLeod returned to

his desk and leaned back in his chair. "What about the other Roth brother? Damien? He wasn't the one originally investigating us, but he's recently been involved. Plus, Russo would owe us for dealing with one of his problems for him. Something strange is going on with the Mariano family right now. This might be a good chance to push our advantage with that den of snakes."

I nearly laughed out loud.

Who was this man to throw shade on the morality of anyone else?

He and David Russo were practically cut from the same cloth. In fact, if I had to choose between the two, I might choose the infamous Mafia Boss over the Senator. At least Russo didn't hold an official seat of power in the government.

Ozias shook his head with urgent, jerky motions, like he didn't want to be caught moving for too long. For the first time since entering the office at the top of the building, I noticed that Ozias's gaze kept trailing off to the side toward the boy sleeping on the couch. He seemed distracted, but quickly snapped himself back to attention to answer the Senator's question.

"There was no sign of Damien Roth, and as far as I can tell, he doesn't have any personal connection to these two."

"Pity." The Senator tapped his fingers on the arm of his chair. "Still, we can at least get rid of one headache. I've already sent someone out to take care of Sebastian Roth and his FBI protector, so you'd better hope your assessment is correct, Ozias. I'll be very disappointed if these two don't turn out to be as useful as you've promised."

"They will be," Ozias instantly promised. "I'm certain of it."

Silence fell between the two men, each waiting for the other to say or do something. The tension hung so heavy between them it seemed to reach right down my throat and steal the air from my lungs.

I pressed closer to Newt, pretending it was to comfort my friend since he hadn't stopped trembling, but I knew it was just as much to comfort myself.

Finally, Senator McLeod smirked. "I suppose you're waiting for your reward, aren't you Ozias? All right. You've done a lot of work for us recently. As promised, you can have your pick of the dolls. We've got a wide selection on the island right now."

I nearly vomited on the spot when I saw that Ozias was so eager and excited for what Senator McLeod offered that he actually started playing with his belt buckle.

He pointed to the boy on the couch. "Him. I want that one."

The Senator's grin twisted into something a little more sinister around the edges. If asked to describe it, I wouldn't be able to pinpoint exactly what changed in his expression from one moment to the next. It was almost as if the very shadows in the room bled into the lines of his face.

"Bold of you to ask for my doll."

He stood again and stepped over to the couch. He stroked his hand over the boy's head, ruffling downy hair just enough to make the boy stir in his sleep but not wake him. "You have good taste. This one is my personal favorite."

Ozias also seemed to pick up on the Senator's changed mood, for he dropped his arm to his side and started messing with his belt buckle again. This time, the gesture seemed less eager and more like a nervous tick.

The Senator's hand left the boy's head to instead trace the ring of bruises around one thin wrist. His fingers aligned perfectly with the dark splotches on tender skin.

"Maybe, if you keep being so useful to us, I'll let you watch while I play with this one. But, no. This doll is mine. Pick a different one. Although, if this is your type, I can make a few recommendations."

Ozias nodded again, but the motion was much smoother than before. "I guess I was hoping for too much. Things are never so easy."

It was an odd statement, but before anyone could say anything in response, three quick popping sounds echoed through the room. The noise was too sudden for me to even jump in surprise and it took me a moment to realize what I was seeing. Once I did, however, my eyes nearly fell out of my skull.

Ozias stood at the center of the room, his arm raised, with the world's smallest gun clenched in his hand.

A weapon small enough to hide inside a belt buckle.

Senator McLeod lay slumped on the

floor, with his bodyguards only a few steps away in a similar position. All three had identical holes in their heads, each less than an inch wide.

The bullets may have been small, but they got the job done. Senator McLeod and his bodyguards were dead.

Ozias's knees made a painfully loud sound against the floor when he collapsed, clinging to the edge of the desk for support as he laughed to himself.

"It worked. Ha ha. Oh god. It worked. Barely had enough bullets, but it's done." He was babbling to himself and barely seemed to realize what he was saying.

I stared in confusion between the man, the gun he'd dropped, and the three newly dead bodies.

"What the hell is going on?"

That seemed to finally snap Ozias out of his stupor. He grabbed the now empty gun off the floor and shoved it back into the hidden compartment in his belt buckle.

"Right. This is... um..."

Before he could get any farther in his explanation, a small voice interrupted him.

"Oz?"

GABE

The boy on the couch had woken up, probably startled by the sound of gunfire, and now his heartbreakingly large eyes were locked onto Ozias.

Ozias rushed toward the boy.

Newt pushed himself to his feet as if to stop the man, but I blocked my friend from interfering. At first, Newt looked at me, confused, but I merely shook my head.

I wasn't sure what was going on, but one thing was clear. The boy not only knew Ozias's name, but even had a nickname for him. They must know each other.

This fact was made even more obvious when Ozias scooped the boy up into a hug, calling his name in turn.

"Milo."

The boy, apparently named Milo, clung to Ozias like an octopus, wrapping all four limbs around the man and holding on with all the strength in his young body.

It was a heartwarming scene, marred only by the fact that I had no idea what it all meant. I hated to interrupt, but there were several very important issues that needed to be addressed.

"Yeah. Excuse me. Two questions.

One. What the hell is going on? And two. Can you untie us?"

I gestured with my bound hands as best I could to draw attention to them while also nodding toward Newt's ropes.

Ozias wiped tears from his eyes without letting go of Milo. "Of course. I'll explain in a moment. Let me find something to cut those ropes."

He kept Milo's head tucked against his shoulder as he stepped over the bodies on the floor and started rifling through the desk.

As we waited to be freed, Newt nudged me with his shoulder and leaned over to whisper in my ear. "I thought that kid was Tansie Bell's son?"

I studied Milo for a moment. It was definitely the same kid from the picture that Tansie Bell had shown us.

"Well, she thought it was her son since he apparently looks just like her ex that got her pregnant, but there was no way to actually confirm it. Either Ozias knows Miss Bell and has also been looking for her son, or she was wrong and the kid was never her son to begin with."

After a few minutes of searching, Ozias managed to find a pocketknife in one of the desk drawers, which he used to cut Newt and I free.

I stood from the blood-splattered floor and rubbed my sore, chafed wrists. Three dead bodies lay at our feet, which I was desperately trying not to think about. I felt no remorse for them. These people definitely deserved to die, but I'd also never been this close to such a fresh corpse.

Instead of focusing on the triple murder I'd just witnessed, I regarded Ozias with a critical eye instead. The man no longer seemed like an immediate threat, but I wasn't willing to immediately trust him.

"All right. We're free. Now explain."

Ozias stared down at Milo, who seemed content to just keep his head buried against the man's shoulder. "I'm not even sure where to start."

"The beginning." I snapped my fingers, drawing the man out of whatever memories he'd fallen in. "Come on. We're in the middle of a swamp stuck on a pedophile's secret dream island. We don't have all day to sit around, and I need to know if we can trust you. So, what's your deal? Why are you here?"

Newt grabbed my arm, silently asking me for patience, but I didn't have much to spare. I was so ready for this whole ordeal to be over.

With a sigh, Ozias placed a hand over Milo's head and lowered his voice to a whisper. "It started two years ago. A friend of mine died. Natural causes. They were sick. Their only family was their little brother. Because of the age gap, they were raising their brother more like a son."

If Ozias was lying, then he was a damn good actor, because the pain on his face looked incredibly real.

"When my friend died, I promised to look after their brother, but I failed. Milo was put into foster care while the courts figured out what to do with him. By the time I managed to get custody, he'd disappeared."

Based on all the information I'd learned from Gabe and Sebastian's investigation, I could already picture what had happened.

"A young kid in the system with no living family. He probably seemed like an easy target that no one would miss."

Ozias's lip pulled back over his teeth

like he was about to bite someone. "Well they fucked up, because I did miss him. It took everything I had, but I managed to track down what happened to Milo. When I realized who had him I tried to go to the police, but..."

"But they were no help," I finished the sentence for him, having already heard similar sentiments so many times before. "Probably paid off to look the other way."

My own blood started boiling from the thought, and I was ready to start biting people right alongside the man.

Newt moved between us, acting like a small ginger wall, and gave a pointed look toward Milo to remind us to keep calm. "I'm sorry to hear about your friend, Ozias, but that doesn't explain what you're doing here. Why are you working for these people?"

"Isn't it obvious." Ozias gripped Milo a little tighter. "If the police weren't going to help, then I would have to get Milo back on my own. It took two years, but I managed to worm my way into their inner circle. Helping to kidnap you was the last hurdle to earning my way here. I wasn't expecting to find Milo so quickly, but I'm not complaining."

Newt stepped closer to the man. "Well, I'm glad our kidnapping could at least accomplish something positive."

However, before he could get too close, I pulled him back to my side. "Hold on. That's a sad story and everything, but I still have one question. This is a secret organization of pedophiles and child abusers. How, exactly, did you convince them that you were one of them?"

If my implication wasn't clear just from my words, the distrustful gaze would have made things easy to understand.

Ozias stumbled back a step, though he never lost his grip on Milo. His face twisted into an expression of shame and disgust that was painful just to look at and he seemed to cave in on himself.

"It actually wasn't that hard." His words were so small, I had to strain to hear them. "All I had to do was say that I prefer to play with dolls that are... complacent, and the kids were kept so drugged up they had no idea what was happening. Or, not happening, in this case."

He started laughing, and I almost smacked the man for making a joke out of something so serious, until I noticed the manic look in his eye.

"But I still have those memories in my brain. All the kids I didn't help who now think I hurt them. Some of the things I've seen. Ha ha… I'm definitely going to need therapy after this." His hands trembled as they formed fists in the fabric of Milo's shirt.

Mental trauma often went hand in hand with physical trauma. I'd seen enough patients in my time who struggled with both to recognize a man who was barely keeping himself from falling apart. While I still wanted to push for more answers—his story was worryingly vague and I still didn't fully trust him—I could also tell that talking about it any more would probably break the man.

Instead, I decided to let it go for now.

I still wasn't sure what to think of everything. So much had happened in such a short amount of time, my brain was struggling to keep up. A part of me still felt like it was back at the fundraising carnival, looking for anything suspicious worth investigating. Or better yet, back at the safe house, waking up next to Gabe and planning out that day's physical therapy session for Sebastian.

At least it was clear that Ozias wasn't our enemy. We already had enough enemies. It was a relief to cross at least one name off the list.

My gaze trailed back to the dead bodies on the floor. We could actually cross several names off our list of enemies, including one very big name. The man who was in charge of the pedophile ring that was hunting us lay dead at our feet, no longer a danger to anyone.

With Senator McLeod dead, what did we do now?

I didn't realize I'd asked the question out loud until Ozias tossed me something. In the few moments while I'd been lost in thought, he'd managed to regain his composure. If I didn't know better, I'd think he was perfectly fine.

I caught the small object as it arched through the air toward me and held it up to the light for a better view.

It was one of the GPS camera pins Newt and I had been wearing.

"I reactivated it shortly after you were kidnapped," Ozias said. "Sorry about that, by the way. I wish there had been another option, but they only reveal the location of this place to people who have *earned* it."

I handed the GPS pin to Newt so he could see it for himself. "No, I get that. But why are you returning this pin to us now?"

Ozias heaved a sigh and sat on the couch, careful not to move the boy more than necessary.

"The Senator may be dead, but this place is still crawling with security. To put it bluntly, there's no way we're getting out of here on our own. We're going to need help."

In his arms, Milo looked like he was halfway asleep again. It was concerning. With all the excitement happening right now, the boy shouldn't be so tired.

A little thought niggling in the back of my brain made me wonder if Milo had been drugged to keep him under control, just like Ozias had described earlier, but I didn't ask.

What could we do even if the boy had been drugged?

He needed medical care either way.

Getting out of here as soon as possible was the best option for everyone.

Newt cupped the GPS pin in both hands like he was holding a small bird, and stared at it the same way he would stare at an interesting puzzle that needed solving.

"Senator McLeod said he sent someone to take care of Sebastian and Gabe."

Technically, what Newt said was a statement, but the question was clear in his tone nonetheless.

"He did," Ozias agreed. "But if your men are half as impressive as they seem, then I'm sure that they'll be fine. They're probably on their way here right now."

I certainly hoped so, because what Ozias said was true. We were going to need help getting out of there. I had plenty of faith in Gabe and Sebastian's abilities and had seen them survive more than one life-threatening situation before.

Yet, I still couldn't help but worry, and from the look on Newt's face, I could tell he felt the same way.

Newt slapped the corner of the desk, like a judge bringing down his gavel on a final decision. "We can't just sit around and wait to be rescued. We may not be able to leave on our own, but there's got to be something we can do in the meantime."

For the first time, I took a good look

around the room. "This was Senator McLeod's personal office in the building, right?"

I looked to Ozias for confirmation, but the man just shrugged. "Maybe. It looks that way, but this is also my first time here, so I don't know for sure."

Newt seemed to catch on to my train of thought and started opening the drawers of the desk. "If this is his personal office, then there's got to be something worth investigating. Information. Computer files. Something we can collect as evidence against this whole operation. We need to make sure that everyone involved pays for what they've done, and that this whole ring gets taken down."

Ozias stood from the couch so quickly he woke up Milo, but the boy quickly settled back to sleep.

"I didn't go through all of this trauma and risk going to prison for killing a Senator just to let the rest of these monsters get away. You go search over there. I'll start with these filing cabinets."

We each took a section of the room. Newt searched the desk, and Ozias took the cabinets, while I turned my attention to the bookcase.

At first, I thought my part of the effort was useless. There was nothing helpful about the bookcase. Even the books themselves seemed like an odd collection of topics that had been thrown together for the sake of aesthetic rather than useful information.

But then, as I was tracing my fingers along the leather bound spines, I noticed something odd.

"Hey, none of these spines are cracked. They're all brand new."

I didn't look over at the others, but I heard them stop whatever they were doing behind me.

"So what?" Newt asked. "It's not illegal to own new books."

"No." I pulled out one of the books. It crackled when I opened it, meaning it had literally never been opened before. "But a collection of books is never entirely new. It's like they were bought all at once and then just placed here for the sake of decoration."

I pulled out a few more books, all equally unopened, and knocked my knuckles against the back of the bookcase.

A hollow echo rattled the wood.

"Bingo. It's a false wall."

Once I knew what I was looking at, it wasn't hard to figure out how to open the bookcase. All I had to do was find the hinges hidden along one side and swing the whole thing open like a door.

On the other side was a small room, just large enough for a desk and an impressively sleek-looking computer.

"Not just bingo. It's a jackpot," I called to the others. "That computer has got to have some important information on it. Newt, you know more about this stuff than I do. Can you take a look?"

"I'll try," Newt said as he stepped through the hidden doorway into the little room. "But playing video games doesn't make me a hacker. If the computer is password protected, we're screwed."

"Just do what you can?"

I watched him for a moment as he booted up the computer, careful about what buttons he hit in case he accidentally triggered some sort of security system.

"Hey, guys," Ozias called from where he stood near the main doorway. "Do you hear that?"

Leaving Newt to figure things out on

his own, I stepped over to the main door. "Hear what?"

Ozias pressed his ear against the door. "That. I think someone's coming up the stairs."

I also pressed my ear to the door. Sure enough, I could hear the faint sound of footsteps. It was surprisingly loud, like the person was trying to make as much noise as possible.

Or maybe they just didn't see any reason to be quiet.

"If they come in here and see all this..." Ozias gestured to the three bodies still lying on the ground. "We're dead."

"Maybe," I agreed. "But if that's the case I'm not going down easily."

Searching the rapidly cooling bodies, I found a gun that was small enough for me to handle and grip it tightly in both hands.

Ozias stepped out of the way as I took a position at the center of the room and pointed the gun at the door. I had no idea what I was doing, but if anyone tried to attack us, I was determined not to hesitate.

CHAPTER TWENTY-THREE

Gabe

THE COOL METAL of the gun warmed slowly as it pressed against the back of my head. Raising my hands, I cautiously turned around.

Tansie Bell stood behind me, gun held in one hand, which she had to angle upward in order to reach my head. She wasn't alone either. Several other heavily armed men stood around her. Their weapons weren't drawn, yet, but it was obvious that one wrong move from me would have me riddled with bullets in less than a second.

"Miss Bell?" I said, trying to pour as

much meaning and question into those two words as I could.

The gun in her hand shook. "I'm sorry, but I have no choice. They have my son. And now they've got your people as well. Those two young men. What are their names? Newt and Frankie? Here."

With the hand not holding a gun, she showed me her phone. On the screen, there was a picture of Frankie and Newt lying unconscious in the back of some sort of vehicle. I only saw the picture for a few seconds, just long enough to identify Newt and Frankie, but not enough to pick out any other details from the photo.

She stored the phone back in her pocket one-handed, while the armed men around her never even twitched.

"They've got your guys just like they've got my son. So, just do what they say. Okay? Please don't make me shoot you."

"All right." I relented, raising my hands back into the air where everyone could see them. "What do you want me to do?"

Tansie hesitated, like she was reading through a list in her mind.

"First, you have to take us to Sebastian Roth. We know he's around here somewhere."

GABE

The demand was expected and didn't take me by surprise. It wasn't the first time I'd been held at gunpoint, though I could admit it was the first time I'd felt afraid.

Not for myself. My high probability of getting killed one day was something I'd accepted a long time ago. However, this time there was more to lose.

If I died now, what would happen to the others?

What would happen to Frankie?

Determined to stay alive, I played along for the moment.

"Sebastian is this way," I said and led them out through the building's cargo bay.

When we stepped out onto the street, Tansie put her gun away. We all knew she didn't actually need it. If anyone was going to shoot me, it would be one of the other armed men silently following us. I counted at least three different concealed weapons on each of them.

Plus, even without any weapons, the threat to Frankie and Newt would be enough to keep me obedient.

To reach the RV where I'd left Sebastian, I would need to turn right and head several blocks down the street.

As a test, I turned left instead.

They didn't correct me, meaning they probably didn't know where Sebastian actually was. That gave me a little room to maneuver and hopefully, regain the upper hand.

"So, what's the end goal here?" I asked as Tansie walked beside me on the street. The armed men watched us both. "Once I give you Sebastian, then what?"

Tansie looked over her shoulder at the men following us. "They're going to kill Sebastian Roth. He's been too much of a thorn in their side to let him live, but you're an agent with the FBI. That could be useful to them."

"Ah. I see." In my head, I reviewed a map of the area. There was a parking deck up ahead that would be perfect for my needs. "They'll keep Frankie and Newt alive so long as I act as their mole."

Silence was more natural to me than conversation, but silence wouldn't do me any good at that moment. Trying to channel as much of Frankie's attitude as I could, I gave my best conceited laugh.

"It seems I was giving your masters too much credit. They aren't as smart as I thought they were."

Beside me I saw Tansie flinch and several of the men following us reached for their guns.

Tansie tugged nervously at one of her pigtail braids.

"Don't... don't say things like that. You'll get us both in trouble. Don't you care if your boyfriend dies?"

Boyfriend?

Is that what Frankie was to me?

The term sounded so juvenile and shallow.

"I'm just surprised," I said as I led our little group into the parking deck and up the long staircase to the top floor. "They've got such a big operation. I assumed they were smarter. Any idiot could tell you that trying to make me their mole in the FBI isn't going to work after you tried to frame me for the Director's death. Even if I'm cleared of the charge, I'll probably be fired anyway."

We'd reached the top floor of the parking deck, which was open to the dreary spring sky.

As soon as my feet touched the asphalt, I turned around to face the armed men following us.

"What happened? Did killing the FBI Director not work out like you thought it would? I heard there's been some difficulty choosing a new Director. Was the person you had set up to take the Director's spot not the shoo-in replacement you thought they'd be?"

None of the other men said anything, but I didn't expect them to. These were just goons. They may not even know what I was talking about. However, their master, Senator McLeod, might be listening to the conversation. If I pissed the man off enough, he might order the goons to do something reckless.

Tansie tugged on my arm. "Don't. Please. Just, take us to Sebastian Roth so we can get this over with."

I sighed, but I couldn't blame the woman for wanting to just go along with her orders. Her son's life was on the line, after all.

As I'd hoped, the top floor of the parking deck was mostly empty. No one wanted to leave their car exposed to the elements if they didn't have to.

I led our group to the far corner of the deck and looked around at the empty spots in confusion.

"I left him in the RV right here. He must have moved."

Several of the armed goons seemed to have enough of my acting and drew their weapons. "Enough," one of the goons said as he pulled out a revolver and pointed it at me. "Take us to Sebastian Roth now."

I held out my hands even as I eyed the gun. A revolver was an interesting choice. It was light weight, easily concealed, and didn't leave shell casings behind, but it also had a limited capacity and was harder to aim accurately due to the short distance between the front and rear sights. To choose such a weapon meant the goon had confidence in their ability to shoot accurately and not require many bullets to get a job done.

Not someone I wanted to get into a shootout with. I would have to wait until I was certain I could take this man out quickly.

"I can't take you to someone if I don't know where they are."

Tansie reached out like she wanted to tug on my arm again, but didn't want to get close enough to put herself in front of the gun.

"Can you call him?"

I did, and wasn't surprised when the phone continued to ring without being picked up. Frankie and Newt weren't the only ones wearing a GPS camera pin. I was as well, which means Sebastian would know I'd been taken hostage.

"No luck," I said when the call went to voicemail.

The nearest goon cocked back the hammer on his revolver.

"You'd better figure something out."

We were at an impasse. I couldn't give them what they wanted, supposedly, and they hadn't been given the order to kill me yet.

The nearest goon suddenly doubled over, clutching a gaping wound in the center of his chest. He'd been shot, and based on the angle the bullet must have come from, I knew who'd pulled the trigger.

Unfortunately, the goon wasn't dead. It would likely be a fatal wound, but he still had enough strength to raise his gun.

I removed the weapon from his hand before he had a chance to shoot. Revolvers weren't my favorite weapon, but I knew how to use them just fine, and didn't hesitate to immediately put another bullet between the goon's eyes. The first man hadn't even hit the ground yet when I turned to the second goon.

The fight was quick. I had the advantage of surprise on my side, plus another ally covering me from a distance. It wasn't long before all of the goons lay either dead or unconscious on the floor.

"What did you do?" Tansie shrieked, panicking as she stared wide-eyed at the bodies bleeding at her feet.

"I'm not sure yet." I turned to face the direction the first bullet came from. "I'm assuming you have a plan, correct?"

Sebastian appeared from behind one of the few cars parked on the upper level of the deck. "Of course. I'm not an idiot." He hobbled toward us with a single crutch tucked under his arm. His right leg barely moved, and couldn't even hold his weight for long. Ideally, he needed a pair of crutches, but that would make wielding a gun nearly impossible. So, he'd found a way to make do with only one.

It took away any hope Sebastian had of looking like an actual threat, but I was just happy to see him up on his feet. These were the first steps he'd taken without clinging to the support bar during

Frankie's therapy. Sure, he was now clinging to a crutch, but it was a definite improvement.

I didn't get much time to appreciate the sight of Sebastian walking before Tansie ran up to him. It was that moment when I remembered the gun still clutched in her hand. The armed goons were dead, but technically Tansie was still a threat.

For a moment, the way she held the gun in front of her, it looked like she was going to shoot Sebastian. I couldn't even blame her if she believed killing Sebastian was the only way to save her child.

I was quick on my feet, but I wasn't faster than a bullet, and Sebastian had no hope of running away.

But then, however, instead of pulling the trigger, she broke down crying and fell to her knees.

"Why did you kill them? My son... They have my son. Oh, god. He's probably dead, now."

In his current physical state, Sebastian couldn't kneel down to be on the same level with the woman, so he awkwardly bent at the waist as best he could while still holding onto his crutch in order to place a hand on her shoulder.

"Maybe not. It's likely that Newt and Frankie were taken to the same place that your son was. If we find them, then we may find your son as well."

I grabbed Sebastian's arm before he could fall over.

"Does that mean you know where they are?"

With a smile that was too sharp around the edges to be called a happy expression, Sebastian held up his phone to display a map. "One of their GPS pins came back on line. We can track where they're being taken."

On the screen, a small red dot was moving along the map, following the line of a road. As I'd noticed earlier, Frankie and Newt were in a vehicle. There was no telling where their kidnappers were taking them, but so long as the GPS pin remained active, we could follow them.

The sight of that little red dot filled me with a small sense of relief.

"Let's get going. The RV isn't the fastest vehicle, and I don't want them getting any farther ahead of us than they already are. We can track them so long as they are driving, but if they are put on a plane or something, then we'll have a much harder time."

I knelt beside Tansie and slipped the gun from her hand before she accidentally shot someone or herself. "Miss Bell. We're going now. Just wait for us and we'll get your son back."

As I stood to leave, a pair of delicate hands grabbed my pant leg and held tight to the fabric. "Please," Tansie begged as she looked up at me from the ground. "Take me with you."

I tried to remove her hands as gently as possible, but she had an iron grip on my clothes. "We can't do that. It'll be dangerous."

She pointed an angry finger at Sebastian. "You'll take a cripple, but not me. What? Just because I'm a woman?"

Breathing deep through my nose to calm my irritation, I shot Sebastian a look and tried to silently plead with him to be patient. I could tell the "cripple" comment hurt him, but I also understood Tansie's anger.

I would also hate being told I couldn't help look for the person I cared about while others were allowed to come.

"It's got nothing to do with your gender. You're not trained for this kind of situation."

"Well, too bad. I'm coming." She climbed to her feet and looked around for her gun, only to scowl when she realized I'd already taken in. Instead, she crossed her arms and tried to look as defiant as possible. "You can't stop me from coming. If you try to leave without me, I'll just follow you. Unless you plan to tie me up."

She was obviously talking out of anger, but I could tell the moment she realized that her hypothetical suggestion might actually happen. We could easily restrain her and leave her somewhere if we were determined not to be followed.

As much as I hated bringing another civilian into this mess, I also hated the idea of becoming a kidnapper when I was trying to stop a bunch of kidnappers.

"Fine." I relented. "You can come, but you are staying out of any combat that might happen. And if I tell you to hide, then you hide. Got it?"

"Yes." Her voice sounded confident, but she nervously twisted her hands around her braid.

I already hated this plan, but we forged ahead anyway.

As we made our way back to the RV as

quickly as Sebastian's crutch would allow him to move, I copied the GPS tracker onto my own phone so I could keep track of Frankie and Newt.

The red dot kept moving, and the feeling of hope in my chest burned a little brighter.

CHAPTER TWENTY-FOUR

Gabe

"IS THIS REALLY where we're going?" Tansie asked as she stood on the dock, looking down at the boat we'd just rented.

Well, we called it renting, but really we'd just stolen the boat and left some money behind to make up for the theft. I told myself that we were going to return the boat, so it would be fine, but a small thought in the back of my mind said that promise might prove to be an empty one. There was no telling what kind of situation we were headed toward.

Sebastian struggled his way into the boat and took a seat on the front bow.

"This is where the GPS tracker leads. And unless you know a better way to travel through a swamp, we're taking the boat. Now, get in."

There was no chance of Sebastian steering the boat when he couldn't even stand up on the swaying floor, so the navigation was left to me. We pulled out of the dock as quietly as possible and headed down the waterway. At the moment, the river was clear, but I knew as we traveled farther into the swamplands that our path would become more treacherous.

We had followed the GPS tracker until it came to a stop seemingly in the middle of nowhere. The map didn't show any cities or towns nearby. There wasn't even a hint of any buildings that could be hiding them. Yet, when I looked up the location, I was surprised how quickly I found a name.

Honey Island Swamp.

It was the largest untouched marshland in the United States, spanning over seventy thousand acres. The area was supposed to be protected by the Louisiana Department of Wildlife and Fisheries, but I wasn't surprised by the idea that someone in the department was corrupt. Our enemies already had spies in the FBI, and were led by a corrupt Senator. A simple Wildlife Department wouldn't be hard to control. It would only take one person agreeing to look the other way for the protected land to become a safe haven for depravity.

The sun was already setting by the time we crossed into the thicker vegetation of the swamp. The world seemed to switch from day to night in a matter of minutes, as the dusk sunlight could no longer break through the canopy. Our boat was of medium size, so I had to stay in the deeper water and be careful not to venture too close to the land. Though in the wet terrain of the swamp, land and water often looked like the same thing, and I came precariously close to crashing us a few times.

Luckily, neither Sebastian nor Tansie seemed to realize my mistakes. Both were too lost in their own thoughts, facing the front of the boat like their concentration was the fuel that propelled us forward.

Normally, I enjoyed the quiet, but this silent atmosphere was oppressive. The hushed rustling of the wind through the trees and the ripple of the water seemed to speak of danger around every corner, and every now and then I caught the flash of some animal's eyes in the dark.

It was easy to see why the darkness of human imagination was often captured by these kinds of landscapes. The swamp around us seemed designed specifically to inspire nightmares. Anything could lurk in the murky water below. Each bump against the boat could be something as simple as a tree branch, or as dangerous as a man-eating predator.

Yet there was also a haunting beauty to it.

I remembered my conversation with Frankie about how the other man hated swamps. Some higher power must be laughing at us right now.

How else could I explain the unlikely odds of Frankie being kidnapped and taken to the one kind of place he despises most?

Honey Island. The name was a cruel joke. There was nothing sweet about this place. Perhaps it once embodied its name, but the monsters that chose to use it as their safe haven had forever tainted it.

I didn't bother to look at the clock on

my phone. I didn't want to know how much time was passing. All I needed to know was that the red dot of Frankie and Newt's GPS location was growing closer.

We would be there soon.

I grew restless under my skin. The need for action burned in my veins. Maybe, finally, we could put this whole torturous adventure behind us.

Finally, after far too much time, a building came into view. I shut off the boat while a cluster of trees sticking directly out of the water still mostly concealed us.

The low, squat building looked out of place in a land that seemed forgotten by time. It was too modern, with hard edges and right angles, and clashed with the organic landscape around it.

It was as if the earth itself was saying this place should not exist.

"Why are we stopping?" Tansie demanded when she noticed that I'd cut the engine. "We're almost there. I can see the building."

I crouched low near the front of the boat, and Sebastian did his best to follow my lead. "Exactly. If we can see them, then they can also see us."

Tansie looked between us and the building, measuring the distance. "What do you mean?"

"Look." I pointed to the expansive dock surrounding the building. "There's security. We can't just stroll up to this place. We'll be shot down before we even get close. We'll have to sneak in."

She huffed, but she joined Sebastian and I in our crouch at the front of the boat. "All right. How do we do that?"

I started unstrapping my guns and handed them to Sebastian. There were only two, but it felt like stripping myself naked.

"I'm going to swim over from here and try to take out as much of the outer security as I can. Sebastian, you're going to cover me from a distance and shoot anyone that looks like they're going to sound an alarm. Tanise, when I give the signal, you'll have to bring the boat to the dock without starting the engine."

She was pulling at her braid again, digging her fingers into the twisted ribbons of hair and pulling them apart at the edges. If this kept up, she was eventually going to make herself bald.

"How am I supposed to move the boat

if I can't turn it on? Get out and push?"

From the boat's storage compartment under the seats, I pulled out a long pole. It was usually used for hooking things that had floated too far away in the water, or pulling someone to safety that was struggling to swim, but it would work for this purpose as well.

"Use this to push off the bottom. You don't need to move fast, and the water current will help once you get started. Just try to stay as silent as possible."

Once I'd removed all my weapons that could be damaged by water, as well as my outer jacket, I slipped into the water armed only with a serrated combat knife. The water was thick with floating vegetation and muck. Great for keeping me hidden, but terrible for visibility.

Not to mention the goosebump-inducing feeling of pond scum sliding against my skin and sticking to my hair.

I swam right up under the dock and clung to a moss-covered support pole. Above me, the footsteps of patrolling security echoed against the wooden boards. I waited until they passed, then climbed up the nearby ladder that dipped down into the water. Each move I made caused the wooden planks to creak, and I kept a cautious eye out for anyone who might spot me.

The first security person was surprisingly easy to take out. I slipped through the shadows until I stood right behind them, then slit their throat between one breath and the next. They collapsed with only a gurgling sound to mark their passing, and I caught them before they could hit the deck and make too much noise.

Once certain that I hadn't alerted anyone, I gently lowered their body into the swamp water below. Their heavy tactical gear weighed them down, so they sank beneath the surface with little effort. Any evidence of their body was swallowed by the floating vegetation, leaving behind only a small spattering of blood on the dock to mark the fact that they once lived.

The process was repeated two more times without anyone noticing anything strange. It felt like the swamp itself was trying to help me cleanse the area, eagerly devouring every enemy I fed to it.

If the swamp was a living nightmare, then it was at least a nightmare that was on our side.

GABE

There were a few times where I couldn't get into position to eliminate my target and had to hide instead by ducking back under the dock. This tactic kept me concealed for the moment, but it wouldn't last forever. Someone was bound to realize what was happening sooner or later.

As much as I wanted to kill everyone within the building for their role in perpetuating this nightmare, I had to remind myself of our purpose. We were there to rescue those who had been kidnapped. Later, we could come back with a larger force and take everyone else out. Surely, now that I knew where they were located, it wouldn't be that hard to rally others willing to help out.

When I'd managed to clear all the security in one section of the dock, I signaled for Tansie to bring the boat closer.

The sound of her moving the pole through the water could barely be heard over the natural ambiance of the swamp. She moved carefully, taking my warning to heart and never letting the pole splash in the water or knock against the side of the boat.

Once they were docked and the boat secured, Sebastian immediately handed me my guns back. With practiced ease, I reattached their holsters on my belt and my leg, then helped Sebastian clamber out of the boat onto the dock. I practically had to carry the man since there was no good way for him to maneuver his crutches without making noise, and even once he was on the dock, I kept one arm looped around him so he leaned more on me than on his crutch.

"Come on," I hurried Tansie out of the boat. "We can't afford to be caught in the open. This dock would be a terrible place for a shootout. There's no cover."

There was a door on the side of the building that looked like it was meant for loading and unloading supplies. The good thing about a secret building in the middle of the swamp was that there wasn't much infrastructure. The whole place looked like it had probably been built by hand, and definitely wasn't up to code. Because of that, the door was ridiculously easy to open. I didn't even have to pick the lock. Ramming it with my shoulder was enough to break the lock and nearly took the door off its hinges.

GABE

This place definitely relied more on secrecy to keep it safe, rather than state-of-the-art security.

Sebastian was through the door first, which led to some sort of storage room. "Come on," he said as he peered through another door that led into the heart of the building. "There's no one around right now, and I can see the staircase. Now's our chance."

He started to slip out the door, but Tansie grabbed his shoulder, stopping him. "How do you know we need to go upstairs? This floor of the building is much bigger. Isn't it more likely that they are down here?"

Careful not to move too quickly or come across as aggressive, Sebastian removed her hand from his arm. "It's hard to build on unstable ground in a swamp like this. Adding a second story would be even harder. If they went through the trouble of creating a second story, then whatever is up there must be important. Probably private rooms, or some sort of center of command. Even if the people we're looking for aren't there, it's the best place to start."

He tried to charge ahead, but this time

I stopped him. "I agree with checking the upper floor, but maybe you should stay here and keep an eye on things."

Sebastian didn't bother to hide his glare as he scowled at me. "I'm not staying behind. What kind of bullshit is that? Newt could be up there."

"That staircase is the only way up," I said, glancing pointedly at his leg. Unfortunately, he didn't take the hint and I had to say it out loud. "You can barely walk. There's no way you're climbing a full set of stairs."

Standing as straight as his crutch would allow, Sebastian shoved his way through the door. "Newt might be up there. I'm going. See if you can stop me."

Sighing deeply and preparing for the worst, I followed after him with one hand poised near my gun at all times.

To Sebastian's credit, he did manage to climb the stairs through a series of odd peg-leg limping and one-legged hopping. He would first brace his bad leg on the step above. Then he would get his crutch firmly planted and quickly hop up with his good leg so his injured one never had to bear his weight for long.

The process worked, but it wasn't

quiet.

It was already a miracle that he was getting around as well as he was, mostly due to sheer determination.

I helped him as much as I could, acting as a second crutch and keeping him on his feet when he nearly tumbled back down the stairs several times. Yet, I knew there was no way our journey up the stairs had gone unnoticed. Even the worst security guards, like the kind often portrayed in cartoons for the sake of comical slapstick, would have heard us coming. When we got to the top of the stairs, I expected to be met with weapons and violence.

Yet, we found nothing but an empty hallway and closed doors.

My stomach twisted with dread. It was too quiet, and we were making our way through the building too easily. Something was wrong.

The hallway had a few doors, but one was obviously more important than the others based on the way it was positioned as the center of attention. Just to be sure, we checked the two smaller doors to reveal a supply closet and a small, thankfully empty, bedroom.

The three of us huddled around the outside of the last door. When I put my ear up to the surface, I could hear faint movement inside. Someone was definitely there, but they weren't making enough noise for me to tell what they were doing.

There was no way to open the door without being noticed. Our only chance would be to burst inside quickly and take out whoever was inside before they could react.

At least Sebastian didn't try to fight me on entering the room first. With a silent nod of acknowledgment, he positioned himself beside the door where he could quickly turn the knob and get out of the way.

With gun in hand, I silently counted to three. Sebastian turned the handle with the hand not clutching his crutch and I kicked the door open.

Inside, I found a rather boring looking office with three people standing around. Looking down the sight of my gun, I found a familiar face on the other end.

"Frankie?"

"Gabe?"

We both immediately lowered the guns we'd been pointing at each other, too stunned to do anything more than stare for a moment.

Our shock was interrupted when Sebastian barreled past me into the room.

"Newt!"

A pair of equally familiar blue eyes peered around an opening in the wall that seemed to lead to a small, attached room. At the sound of his name, Newt stepped into the open and wrapped his arms around Sebastian as the two of them practically fell against each other.

Whispered words were passed back and forth in their embrace, but I couldn't hear what they said. Although, I wasn't trying to listen anyway. I was too busy staring at Frankie, who was nervously scratching at the back of his head.

"Sorry about…" He vaguely waved the gun around, then realized what he was doing and set the weapon down on the desk. "You know. Almost shooting you. That would have been a bad reunion."

He started laughing, but was cut off as I pulled him into a tight hug.

"Don't do that again," I said as I buried my face against his hair.

"What? Almost shoot you?"

"No. Don't get kidnapped again."

Frankie wrapped his arms around my waist and held tight enough that I would probably have bruises there tomorrow. "I'll try, but getting kidnapped wasn't really a choice. Otherwise, I would have chosen differently. It's not an experience I recommend."

Pulling away from the hug just enough to look him in the eye, I searched him for any sign of injury. I didn't see anything, but that didn't mean there weren't hidden wounds I couldn't see.

"Are you all right? Did they hurt you?"

Frankie leaned his head against my chest, so my shirt muffled his words. "One of the security guys held my head under the water. Like I didn't need any more reason to hate swamps. It was gross. And terrifying. I'm never going anywhere near a swamp ever again."

Rage boiled under my skin at the thought of anyone laying a violent had on the other man. As much as I wanted to run off and kill every member of the building's security, I also didn't want to let Frankie go.

In the end, the desire to keep Frankie in my arms won out and I stayed right where I was.

GABE

"I killed a few people on the way in here and dumped their bodies in the water. Maybe the person who hurt you was one of them."

Frankie laughed until he cried. The tears didn't seem like happy ones, but I didn't say anything as I continued to hold him.

A clatter of metal and wood caught my attention. Sebastian's leg had apparently reached its limit and Newt was helping him sit on the desk. His crutch had banged against the furniture since he refused to let go of Newt, resulting in an ugly tangle of limbs.

Finally able to concentrate on more than just my relief at seeing Frankie alive, I took a better look around the room and flinched when I recognized the third person standing just a few feet away.

"Ozias Wren?"

I had my gun in my hand and pointed at the man before his name had even finished leaving my mouth.

Yet, to my surprise, Frankie grabbed my arm and forced it back to my side.

"No, wait, Gabe. It's okay. He's on our side."

I looked away from Ozias just long

enough to raise an eyebrow in Frankie's direction. "What do you mean he's on our side? He's working for the Senator."

Rather than answer, Frankie just pointed at the floor. It was a testament to how distracted I was that I didn't notice the bodies lying on the floor. Two of them looked like bodyguards, while one was definitely Senator McLeod.

"What happened?"

"It's a long story. But, like I said, Ozias is on our side. He's not a threat."

I was still struggling to process what Frankie was saying. "You mean he killed the Senator?"

"Yeah, in order to... oh. What's Miss Bell doing here?"

Frankie was staring at Ozias with concern.

I followed his gaze to see Ozias standing off to the side of the room with a familiar boy in his arms.

Ozias and Tansie stared at each other, each with an unreadable expression on their faces.

"Who're you?" Ozias demanded as he held the boy closer and backed up a step. "What do you want?"

Tansie said nothing as she stared at

the boy with a dozen different thoughts racing behind her eyes and her fists twisting at one of her braided pigtails.

Frankie pulled out of my arms and approached her with his hands held out in front of him like he was trying to sooth a frightened animal.

"Um, Miss Bell. Let me explain. There's a lot to talk about."

"No," she said with a voice that sounded like it came from a completely different voice box. "There's nothing to talk about."

CHAPTER TWENTY-FIVE

Frankie

A SHARP PAIN cutting across my neck was my first warning that anything had happened. I never saw Tansie move, but in the blink of an eye she was standing behind me and I suddenly couldn't breathe.

"Frankie," Gabe shouted, sounding more distressed than I'd ever heard him.

Yet, it was as if everything were happening too fast for my emotions to keep up, so they'd just decided to shut down. A deeply ingrained instinct told me to keep my head still, so I looked around using only my eyes.

Gabe, Newt, and Sebastian were all looking at me terrified. Tansie stood pressed up against my back. One of her braids was undone, and I could just see the messy rope of hair in my peripheral.

Her hands hovered near each of my shoulders, holding tight to a wire that was wrapped around my neck.

Had she been hiding the wire in her hair the whole time?

That was a smart idea. I also had long braids. Maybe I should start doing the same thing.

Like a drowning man clinging to a single piece of driftwood, I couldn't stop thinking about the logistics of hiding a wire in my own hair. It was easier than facing the reality of my situation.

Tansie had a sharp garrote wire wrapped around my neck. Assuming she knew how to use such a weapon, one quick snap of her hands would kill me.

"Miss Bell, what are you doing?" Newt demanded. He tried to come closer, but Gabe and Sebastian both stopped him.

Gabe eyed her with a narrow look, glancing briefly at the boy in Ozias's arms like he was stitching pieces of a tapestry together.

GABE

"You've been telling us that this boy is your son, but that was a lie, wasn't it. Do you even know him at all?"

Tansie didn't answer, but she didn't have to. Ozias's response said everything.

He held the boy closer, and back up until his shoulder hit a wall. "What? She's got nothing to do with Milo. I've never even heard of this woman."

Since she was standing behind me, I couldn't see her, but the venom in Tansie Bell's voice made her sound like a completely different person.

"So, you're the one who's fucked everything up. As soon as that GPS tracker went back online, I knew something had gone wrong, but I never suspected you. Good job. You might be a better actor than I am."

Fuck.

It was all a trap.

We should have known.

It seemed like everywhere we turned someone was trying to get one over on us. No one could be trusted. Not even a seemingly innocent woman desperate to find her missing son.

Tansie tugged on the wire around my neck. "Get moving. Back up. Nice and slow."

The wire bit into my neck as I walked backward with her one step at a time. A drop of blood rolled down my neck, leaving a warm path on my skin, but it wasn't deep enough to do any real damage yet. Skin damage and muscle damage felt different, and I'd experienced enough of both to know the differences.

Focusing on my feet and trying not to trip as she led me out the office door, kept the panic at bay. Once we were out the door, Tansie ordered me to lock everyone else inside.

"I-I don't have a key."

Panic was starting to catch up to me. I could feel it like hot metal in the back of my throat.

If I was separated from the others, how long would I last?

I wasn't a fighter, and my value as a hostage would disappear the moment Tansie was safe.

I needed to get away from her, but Tansie merely laughed at my attempt to stall for time.

"You don't need a key. I know what you can do. If you can open a lock without a key, then you can re-lock it as well."

How did she know about that?

As far as I knew, she'd never seen me pick a lock.

How long had this woman been watching us?

Gabe and the others shouted in protest, but they didn't dare take a step closer as another drop of blood rolled down my neck.

Breathing deeply through my nose, I pulled the lock picks I'd brought out of my pocket and locked the office door.

Only the two of us remained in the hallway, but Tansie still didn't let me go. The wire remained securely around my neck as she led me down the stairs back toward the dock, always keeping me in front of her like a human shield.

"You don't have to do this," I said as I carefully navigated the stairs. "Senator McLeod is dead. Your operation won't survive without its leader. There's no point in fighting anymore."

Tansie just laughed at me as she kicked open the door leading out of the building with her foot.

Outside, at least a dozen security personnel waited for us, each as heavily armed as the next.

Her breath brushed over my skin as she spoke directly into my ear. "Senator McLeod certainly does seem like the kind of person you'd expect to run this place." Every member of security snapped to attention as soon as they noticed Tansie and me. "You and your friends have been in hiding so long, I thought you'd have figured it out a little better. If you want to go unnoticed, then you've got to give people what they expect to find so they stop looking."

Well… fuck.

The nearest security personnel saluted Tansie.

"Ma'am. What's going on?"

"There are intruders locked in the main office. Go take care of them. Then start getting everything ready for relocation. This location may have been compromised."

As soon as they had their orders, her goons sprang into action. Half of them immediately ran upstairs to deal with Gabe and the others. A few more headed off in a different direction, probably to start the "relocation process."

I didn't know exactly what that meant,

but I could guess. They would take the children they had and disappear so they could set up again in a whole new location.

Maybe even a whole new country.

It had taken Sebastian and Gabe so much effort to track them down and they had succeeded mostly through luck. If these monsters disappeared now, we'd probably never find them again.

Faint shouting could be heard coming from the upper story of the building. Then gunshots rang out. Every muscle in my body locked up as panic rushed through me. I was truly terrified that I was listening to my friends die.

Yet, as the seconds ticked by, the shouting only grew in volume, and even more gunshots rang out over the bayou. It sounded like a war had broken out just above our heads.

"What is going on?" Tansie shouted.

Her attention shifted to the remaining security personnel as she demanded answers.

The wire around my neck fell slack.

I moved before I even consciously decided to do so. Gabe had taught me many ways to get away from someone holding me against my will, but he hadn't covered how to escape a garrote wire.

So, I improvised.

Throwing my head back, I slammed my skull into Tansie's face. Pain speared my head right in the same spot as my scar and I crumbled to my knees. For a moment, I was eighteen again, and lying in a pool of my own blood in the high school parking lot. I never saw the bat coming for me, but I felt the moment it made contact. Worse, however, was the sound of my attacker laughing as he left me to bleed alone.

However, the memory passed quickly, and I looked up to see Tansie doubled over, screaming in pain as she clutched an obviously broken nose. Blood dripped between her fingers and dribbled down her chin.

My head hurt, but this time I wasn't the one left bleeding.

Tansie's words were garbled as she shouted, but I could understand enough to know she was ordering security to kill me.

Several guns pointed in my direction. I couldn't run. The dock was wide open. There was no way to outrun a bullet.

So, I did the only thing I could. I dove into the swamp water below.

As soon as the murky water touched my skin, I shivered in disgust, but I stayed down long enough to swim under the dock. Although it only took a few seconds, I was already gasping for air when I re-emerged.

Rotted vegetation dripped from my hair into my eyes and I gagged. I already hated swamps, but now they were going to have a starring role in all my future nightmares.

Above the wooden boards of the docks, I could hear more gunfire. Then something heavy landed in the water near me. One of the security personnel stared up at me with vacant eyes before their body sank beneath the surface and disappeared.

Gripping onto the edge of the dock, I pulled myself up and peered over the wood.

Gabe and Sebastian steadily made their way across the dock. They were an army of two, systematically tearing their way through the building's security. Half a dozen bodies lay strewn over the wooden boards behind them, and I had no doubt that there were more inside the building. Although Sebastian still couldn't move very quickly thanks to his crutch, it didn't matter. They were methodical and precise as they disposed of every enemy they came across.

A hollow clicking sound rang across the dock as one of Gabe's guns ran out of bullets. He ducked back behind Sebastian while he reloaded, but with only one free hand, Sebastian couldn't provide as much cover fire as Gabe could.

A pair of heavy boots ran past me as one of the security personnel tried to charge at Sebastian and Gabe while they had a chance.

From my place hidden below the edge of the dock, I reached out and grabbed the charging man's ankles. He tripped and slammed face first into the boards. The echo of his impact with the wood alerted Gabe and Sebastian to his presence.

Gabe quickly finished reloading and shot the fallen man before he could stumble to his feet.

Blood seeped between the cracks of the wooden boards and dripped down into the swamp. Red puddles collected on the dock and stained the cuffs of Gabe's pants with each step he took.

Across the dock, I noticed a figure crawling in the opposite direction. At some point during the gunfight, Tansie had taken a bullet in the leg. She couldn't walk. Instead, she was dragging herself toward one of the boats.

I couldn't help Gabe and Sebastian with their shootout, but this was something I could handle.

Ducking back into the water, I carefully swam to the other side of the dock. Debris brushed against me under the water. I told myself it was just a branch, or a rock, or a particularly thick clump of vegetation. It couldn't possibly be one of the many bodies that had ended up in the water tonight or any of the man-eating beasts I knew resided in the water's depths.

So long as I didn't look, then the truth was whatever I wanted it to be.

I reached Tansie just as she tumbled into one of the boats. There was no way to silently climb into the boat with her, so I didn't even try. She easily saw me coming as I clawed my way out of the water and into the boat with her, but she was in no condition to fight back.

With a closer look, I could see that she'd been shot with more than one bullet. Her right leg was a bloody mess, and I silently cheered when I noticed it was the same leg that Sebastian had injured.

For a moment, as I stood over her dripping water and heaving for breath, I felt like our roles had been reversed. I was the monster, and she was the victim.

Then, I remembered everyone who had been hurt because of her, and the feeling passed.

"Please," she begged, looking up at me with such believable terror. "I didn't want to. They made me do it. Just let me go and you'll never hear from me again."

I was sure my grin showed a little too many teeth as I grabbed one of the boat's oars. "Nice try, but I'm not falling for that again."

The fear disappeared from her face and was replaced with cold indifference. "Worth a shot. Don't suppose I could pay you instead?"

"Not on your life."

Wood met flesh with resounding smack as I struck her over the head with the oar. The blow sent uncomfortable vibrations up my arm, and I held tighter to the oar as I watched her slump over on the bottom of the boat.

She was unconscious, but still alive. I could have killed her, but that one blow felt like it had taken all my energy. My hands shook, and I leaned against the oar for support.

I'd done my part. Someone else could finish the job.

When I finally felt strong enough to stand without using the oar as a crutch, I looked up to find the gunfight on the dock drawing to a close. Only a few security personnel remained, and they were easily dispatched.

The swamp fell silent.

Gabe and Sebastian stood alone, chests heaving, back-to-back in the middle of a dock covered in bodies and bloody puddles.

I waved to get their attention. "Hey. Where's Newt?"

The two of them headed over to me but didn't holster their weapons.

"We left him and Ozias locked in the office to finish getting everything they could off the computers," Sebastian said as he approached. Looking down into the boat, he nodded toward Tansie. "She still alive?"

I climbed out of the boat to join him and Gabe on the dock. "Yeah. What should we do with her?"

Gabe slipped his arm around my waist and pulled me closer. "If we bring her in, then the authorities can build a case against her and everyone who helped her."

"Yeah." Sebastian gave a distracted nod.

Then he raised his gun and shot her, pulling the trigger repeatedly until he ran out of bullets.

"What?" he said when he noticed us looking at him with concern. "After everything she's done to me, not to mention how many kids she's hurt with her part in this thing, there's no way I'm letting her live. I don't care if it means we can't make a case against her. Now, she can't hurt anyone else."

A few months ago, the idea of killing someone while they were unconscious and helpless would have turned my stomach. Now, I just nodded in agreement.

Did that make me a monster?
Maybe.
Did I regret it?
No.

"So now what?" I asked as I turned back toward the building. Sebastian's bullets had punched right through Tansie's body and through the bottom of the boat. Water slowly leaked through the holes and surrounded her, covering her body inch by inch. Eventually, she'd be pulled under the surface and swallowed by the swamp that had once been her safe haven.

It was a satisfying ending for her, but that didn't mean I wanted to stay around and watch. There was too much to do, and I wanted to get out of the swamp as quickly as possible.

Gabe's arm around my waist squeezed tighter for a moment in an awkward side hug. "Hopefully, Newt and Ozias are having luck with the computers. We need to round up the children who are here and get them to safety. Then... we salt the earth and make sure no one can ever use this place again."

Although Gabe made it sound so easy, the whole process took us several hours.

Newt and Ozias were successful in copying everything off the office's computers and disconnected the hard drive to bring with us just in case. Hopefully, that would be enough to make a case against the pedophile ring even without their leader in custody.

The children trapped in the building, however, were a different matter. We first had to find a way to unlock all the doors in that prison hallway I'd noticed earlier. Then, even once the doors were opened, it took some time to convince the children who were locked inside to come out.

I couldn't blame them. Every time their door opened in the past it probably led to more pain. They had every reason to distrust us.

Surprisingly, the fact that several of them recognized Ozias and Milo actually helped. Out of all of us, the children seemed to trust him the most.

Ozias claimed that every time he'd been forced to pretend like he was an active member of the pedophile ring, the child in question had been too drugged to know what was happening. However, I wondered if, in some subconscious part of their minds, the children knew he'd never touched them.

The sun was rising by the time we were finally sailing away from Honey Island. It took several boats to bring all the children with us. Newt and Ozias were going around, checking on the children and trying to keep everyone as comfortable and calm as possible.

I should have been helping them, but I couldn't bring myself to face so many blank stares and empty eyes. The pedophile ring had called them *dolls*, and now I understood why. They seemed empty and fragile, like one wrong move would shatter them to pieces.

None of my physical therapy training had prepared me for this, and I didn't trust myself not to make it worse. These children needed a proper therapist that knew how to help them. My specialty lay in healing the body, not the mind. In this situation, I was as helpless as anyone else.

Instead, I stood next to Gabe and watched as the hidden building in the swamp disappeared.

Gabe's idea to "salt the earth" ended up involving less salt and more fire. Once we were certain that every living person had been cleared out of the building, and we'd gotten as much from the computers as possible, we set fire to the structure.

It ignited surprisingly easily. The building had definitely not been constructed with safety in mind. The dock proved to be especially flammable. Entirely made from wood, despite the moisture all around, it still acted as eager kindling. In only half an hour, a few flames managed to consume the entire building.

As we sailed away, I stood at the back of the boat to watch it all burn. The light of the flames eclipsed the rising sun and brought warmth to such a dank place.

A strange humming filled the air and all the nearby birds and insects swarmed into the air to escape the flames.

Honey Island Swamp sang as it was cleansed by fire. Only ashes would be left behind, but in their wake a new, clean environment could finally grow.

CHAPTER TWENTY-SIX

Frankie

"HAVE YOU BEEN able to contact Damien?"

Gabe's question took Sebastian by surprise, and the man froze in the doorway.

"I managed to get a call through to him on that secure phone Lily gave us," Sebastian said, once he overcame his shock enough to maneuver his crutch through the doorway.

Gabe and I handled the luggage, which wasn't much, so Newt was free to help Sebastian into our temporary apartment.

Sebastian and Damien's apartment

and office had blown up, and now Newt and I had lost our apartment after disappearing for so long without a word. Apparently even the FBI couldn't contend with the greed of a stingy landlord.

At least Newt and I hadn't lost all our stuff. It was being held in a storage locker for us, just waiting to be collected once we figured out where we were staying.

After everything that happened on Honey Island, there was a lot to figure out.

All of the children we rescued had been placed in emergency foster care while their families were located, and the information we'd stolen from the computers had been delivered to the correct people.

Meaning it had been given to Lily, and she determined who the correct people were. At that point, I agreed with Gabe. Lily was the only one in the FBI that I trusted. She may only be a secretary on paper, but in practice she basically ran things.

Hopefully, whoever they promoted to be the new FBI director would be willing to fall in line with this arrangement, or else they may not be the director for long.

GABE

Once inside the apartment, Sebastian collapsed onto one of the many soft looking couches. He was getting around much better than before, but using his crutch still left him tired.

Newt and I both agreed that Sebastian would probably always walk with a limp but based on the progress that he'd made so far, we could probably get him to the point where he would only need a basic leg brace and maybe a cane for support, rather than the bulky crutch. He'd probably even be able to return to his private investigator work, if he wanted. Although, at the moment, all talk of the future was vague at best. We'd all been so focused on surviving, that none of us had given much thought to what we wanted to do after the whole ordeal was over.

Luckily, we had time to figure it out.

The FBI had provided us compensation, as well as a temporary place to stay. They'd actually offered us multiple apartments, but after living in hiding for so long, we all felt more comfortable staying together for now.

Newt took a seat at Sebastian's side, instinctively checking his leg, though it wasn't as necessary now.

"Will your brother be coming back? I know you want to see him."

With a sigh, Sebastian pinched the bridge of his nose while at the same time leaning into Newt's touch.

"I don't know. I told him about what happened, and that we're all alive. He was happy to hear it, but he couldn't talk for long. I think something must be happening with... whatever he's doing because he seemed distracted."

I took a seat on the other couch and pulled Gabe down with me so I could tuck myself under his arm. "I wouldn't be surprised if Damien is even busier now. We burned down the pedophile ring, and Ozias has agreed to go into witness protection to testify against them, but there's nothing stopping the Mariano family from just funding another operation somewhere else."

"That won't happen."

All four of us jumped to our feet at the sound of the unexpected voice.

A man I'd never seen before stood in the doorway, just a few feet away. He was well built, in a lean way, with dark hair and even darker eyes. A silver ring glinted on one eyebrow, complimenting his dark olive complexion.

Just behind him stood the largest man I'd ever seen. He wasn't much taller than Gabe or Sebastian, but his shoulders seemed to go on forever, and he maintained a wide, sturdy stance that seemed specifically designed to take up as much space as possible.

"How did you get in here?" I demanded, while at the same time wondering why no one else was talking. Gabe was usually the silent type, but even he would speak up when needed, and Sebastian was never known for holding his tongue. Yet the two of them stood there in complete silence.

We hadn't even heard the two strangers enter the apartment.

How had they snuck up on us so easily?

As usual, when I was nervous, my attitude made itself known.

"We aren't entertaining guests right now. You'll have to come back later."

I approached them, although I had no idea what I intended to do. However, before I could take more than a single step, Gabe grabbed my arm and pushed me behind him.

Usually, Gabe was careful with his strength, but he gripped me so tight that I could already feel bruises forming.

Any protest I would have made died when I noticed the look on his face. It was a mix of terror and fury that instantly stole my voice.

"Alex Mariano," he said through clenched teeth, as though that single name should answer any questions.

In a way it did. The name Alex wasn't familiar to me, but Mariano definitely was. This man had some connection to the Mafia Boss, and here he was standing in our living room as if he had every right to be there.

"Well, I guess that means introductions aren't necessary," Alex said as he took a seat in the room's only remaining chair.

The other unnamed man stood just behind him, probably acting as a bodyguard. With a better look, I could see a bit of gray at the man's temples, marking him as the oldest person in the room, but I wasn't fooled into thinking that a few more years made him less dangerous. The man carried himself the same as Gabe, like he was a walking weapon just waiting to be aimed at someone.

Alex looked at us expectantly, one leg crossed over the other in a relaxed pose. When no one moved, he gestured toward the couches. "Sit. Let's talk."

Sebastian took a stumbling step forward, nearly tripping on his crutch. "I'm not sitting until you explain what the hell David Russo's son is doing in our apartment. How did you even find us?"

Well, that explained Alex's connection all right. The head of the Italian mafia was so intertwined with Sebastian and Gabe's lives, yet he'd always seemed like more of a myth than a man. I'd never pictured him having a family. Yet, here sat his son, just as flesh and blood as anyone else.

I wasn't sure if that made the Mafia Boss more or less intimidating.

Alex chuckled under his breath. "Finding you wasn't actually that hard."

Gripping his crutch tighter, Sebastian stood a little taller. "Your father has been trying to find my brother and I for years without success."

With a surprisingly playful expression, Alex tipped his head to the side as he looked Sebastian up and down. "My father is… *was* set in his ways. He preferred to rely on his old allies rather than forging new ones. It created certain… blind spots in his influence, which you and your brother have navigated expertly. Well done. I, however, do not have those same blind spots. Now, sit. We have a lot to talk about."

Still, nobody moved, until Gabe unexpectedly spoke up.

"Reyes."

He pointed at the man standing behind Alex, eyes narrowed and mind obviously spinning.

The man stared back.

"Long? Right? You were the medic."

"Garrison?" Alex leaned over to address his bodyguard with an inquisitive raised eyebrow. "You two know each other."

"We served together. Different units, but we went on a few joint missions."

Gabe flinched like he'd just remembered something. "The mission with the camels."

"Those fucking camels," the bodyguard, Garrison, agreed.

The two studied each other for another moment, though this time there was less hostility. Eventually, Gabe nodded and gestured for me to take a seat on the couch.

"All right. We'll hear you out."

"What?" Sebastian started to protest, but Gabe cut him off.

"It won't hurt to talk. They've already found us, so running now wouldn't do us much good."

With some grumbling, and help from Newt to navigate his crutch, Sebastian also took a seat.

"Great." Alex clapped his hands together like this was a brunch meetup with friends and he was about to spill the latest gossip. "First, a show of good faith. I'm here to provide you with Tansie Bell's true identity."

That information would really help with the case against the pedophile ring, and I could tell Gabe was eager to hear it from the way he shifted forward slightly.

Alex seemed to sense the eager atmosphere in the room, for he grinned like a satisfied cat. "Tansie Bell does seem to be her real name, not that it means much. She was sold into human trafficking at a young age and managed to work her way up into a position of power.

We think she did it mainly through blackmail. You'd be surprised what secrets people are willing to admit during pillow talk."

He consulted something on his phone, scrolling through information with a scowl before continuing. "A few years ago, she got pregnant, and that seems to have been the catalyst for her to start her own operation."

"Why..." Newt started to speak, then stopped himself. However, when all eyes turned toward him, he plucked up his courage and kept talking. "Why would getting pregnant inspire her to start her own pedophile ring? That seems... unnatural."

Alex just shrugged. "Perhaps she realized she had easy access to new product? I'm not going to pretend I understand the mindset of these kinds of people. I've always had more... mature preferences." As he spoke, his gaze drifted toward his bodyguard. The heat in his gaze practically undressed the man in front of all of us.

There was no mistaking the nature of their relationship.

"Anyway..." Alex cleared his throat and

tore his gaze away from his bodyguard with obvious reluctance. "Do with that information what you will. It's just a peace offering, and not really why I'm here."

"So, what is your purpose here," Gabe demanded. He draped his arm around my shoulder in a protective position, like he was ready to drag me out of the room at a moment's notice. "If you've had the ability to find us whenever you want, why approach us now? Does your father know you're here, or are you going behind his back?"

I flinched when Alex suddenly started laughing. It was a light and mirthful sound, as though he were truly delighted. Such a genuine expression was unexpected coming from a man in his position.

"At this point, if I wanted to go behind my father's back, I'd need a shovel. He's already dead and buried."

Sebastian shot to his feet, but tripped over his crutch and would have face planted in the carpet if Newt hadn't caught him. "What? How? When?"

"A few weeks ago," Alex said with a dismissive wave of his hand. "Someone killed him, which isn't a surprise. Someone was going to kill him eventually. It was a lovely funeral."

The wicked twist to his grin told me that something had happened at that funeral, and based on the glint in his dark eyes, I probably didn't want to know the details.

"And you're here to…" Sebastian shook his head as he struggled to understand what was going on. "Settle his scores?"

Alex waved a hand in front of his face like he was warding off an offensive smell. "Oh, no. My father's grudges die with him. I'm just here to say… no hard feelings."

"No hard feelings?" Gabe repeated, his voice as cold as I'd ever heard it. "The Roth brothers helped put your father in prison. Your family killed my sister. And you expect us to not have any hard feelings?"

Emotions around the room grew tense, and the bodyguard standing behind Alex let one hand drift toward his gun. The man was on a hair trigger, and I didn't want to see what would happen if that trigger was pulled.

Yet, in contrast to everyone else, Alex still looked completely relaxed as he braced one elbow on the arm of his chair. "My father was foolish enough to get himself arrested. That's on him, and I don't care what role anyone else played in it. He's dead. I'm in charge of the family now, and I have no interest in things that happened a decade ago. As for your sister…"

He paused thinking for a moment as his fingers tapped against his lips. "I honestly know nothing about your sister. If my father had a hand in her death, I'm sorry, but there's nothing I can tell you about it."

Although on the outside Gabe didn't seem to react, I could feel a change in the tension of his body. He didn't relax, but something inside him seemed to unravel.

I stopped paying much attention to what Alex was saying after that. Everything important had already been said. The next ten minutes were filled with repeat assurances that Alex had no intention of coming after any of us, and that the hit on Sebastian and Damien had been canceled.

All of this went right over my head as I focused on Gabe. His reaction worried me, mostly because I couldn't tell what he was thinking. I'd gotten a lot better at reading him since we'd first met, however, this time I was completely out of the loop.

Even a few hours later, after Alex and Garrison had left, and Gabe and I were alone in our new bedroom, I still had no idea what was going on in my lover's head.

We lay together in the king-size bed, still mostly clothed, just listening to the seconds ticking by in silence. It wasn't that long ago that I would have killed for my own bedroom. Yet now we finally had a place with enough space for everyone, and all I wanted to do was share a bed for the rest of my life.

"Hey, Gabe."

I threw a leg over his waist and straddled him, so I was looking down at his face. It was easier than trying to hold a conversation while looking up at him, which I usually ended up doing even when we were lying down.

"Come on, Gabe. Talk to me."

Gabe settled his hands on my hips. It wasn't a sexual move. Just a moment of contact, like Gabe was reminding himself that he wasn't alone.

"I think I need to give up."

That wasn't the reaction I expected, and a cold weight settled in my stomach. "Give up on what?"

He sighed, and his gaze drifted sideways toward the room's only window. "On my sister. On finding her killer. I know the Mariano family was involved, but what's the point in pursuing it now? She died years ago. Alex Mariano would have only been a teenager then. Even if he was somehow involved, he wasn't the one calling the shots. The man responsible for her death is dead now, too. So, I think… I need to give up on getting justice for her."

I laid down so my head was on his chest. Then, using one finger, I turned his chin to make him look at me. "You know, letting something go isn't the same as giving up. There's already so much violence and abuse in the world. Hanging onto things too long doesn't help anyone. It just keeps the cycle going."

I thought back over everything we'd just learned. My brain was so full of information I could hear it buzzing, but a few key facts stood out.

"Like, look at Tansie Bell. She was a victim of human trafficking who eventually became a human trafficker.

The cycle of victim and abuser can be endless if we never learn how to break it." With light fingers I traced the scar on the back of my head. "The person who attacked me will never really pay for it. Not in a way that will ever make up for what he did. It took me a few years, but I eventually learned to live with that and move on."

I held Gabe's gaze for a moment, reading the depth of emotion hidden within that gray color. "So that's the real question. Can you learn to live with it, even if you never get answers?"

Pulling my hand away from my head, Gabe brought it to his mouth and kissed the tips of my fingers. "I think I can learn to let go, so long as I have something new to hold on to."

I grinned and pulled my hand away so I could feel his kiss on my lips instead. "That is something I can provide."

We kissed until I couldn't breathe any more. Until every memory of swamps and blood had been chased from my mind. As our breath mingled, we kept repeating the same promises over and over until it felt like a mantra engraved on our souls.

"Hold onto me."

GABE

"Always."

Dear Reader,

Thank you for reading Gabe & Frankie's story. Can you believe life might actually become normal for Sebastian and Damien now? What a concept! Make sure you click to preorder your copy of Logan, the next book in the Federal Protection Agency series.

Oh, and if you enjoyed this book, maybe you'll do me a huge favor and leave a review. Even a few words would mean the world to me, and it also helps other readers find the stories you love.

Thanks!

~Evie Riley

OTHER BOOKS BY EVIE

Federal Protection Agency
Mason
Rafe
Ryzen
Cooper
Noah
Damien
Sebastian
Gabe
Logan

Ruthless Empire
Courting Danger
Chasing Danger
Kissing Danger

Smokejumpers
Hawke
Cyrus
Jase
Gage
Jackson
Xavier

Jasper Springs
Cade
Dawson
Drew
Grayson
Riley
Mitch

From The Edge
Shattered
Runaway
Jaded
Rescue
Hidden
Tormented

Gray Vale Pack
His Fated Mate
His Wounded Warrior
His Healing Heart

ABOUT THE AUTHOR

Evie Riley is a prolific, neurodivergent author known for her captivating MM romance novels. She has gained a significant following and topped the LGBT+ action and adventure bestseller charts with her series.

Evie's writing style often explores dark and gritty themes where her men must overcome difficult obstacles in their search for love, but she has also ventured into sweeter small-town romances, incorporating tropes like enemies-to-lovers, friends-to-lovers, age-gap, and forced proximity. She is known for crafting engaging romantic suspense novels and has a knack for creating interconnected series worlds that keep readers invested.

Interestingly, Ms. Riley has hinted at exploring new genres, such as Alien Omegaverse Romance, in the future.

Outside of writing, she enjoys spending time at the beach and has a quirky personality, described by her partner as ranging from cute to deadly, depending on her blood-chocolate levels.

Evie spends her nights writing bad boys in love, and her days wrangling the sweet boys she loves.